*F0*1
FESTIVITIES

FOREST FESTIVITIES

by
Mica Ford

First Published in Great Britain in 2018
by Castleman Publishing

ISBN 978 0 9928482 3 1

Typeset at The Spartan Press Ltd,
Lymington, Hants

Printed and bound in Great Britain by
The Dorset Press, Dorchester.

Cover designed by Marion Baylis

Line drawings by Beresford Leavens

FOREST ADVENTURES

Book 1 : Forest Summer
Book 2 : Forest Festivities
Book 3 : Forest Rescue
Book 4 : Forest Rustlers

Facebook : Mica Ford – Forest Adventures

This book is dedicated to the many ponies
and horses who have enhanced
my life and offered me
their trust and love.

1

Beth wondered what had woken her. It was so quiet she could hear her sisters breathing softly but there was no other sound. Even in the middle of the night there was always something going on outside their attic bedroom; traffic, branches brushing against the roof, birds calling, the wind or rain pattering on the windows. But now everything was still with a strange glow coming through the skylights.

Shivering, Beth eased out of bed, grateful she was on the lower bunk so would not wake Niki by climbing over her. She padded over to the window; it was snowing. Normally any self-respecting eight year old would whoop with delight to see snow, but she gasped with horror and ran downstairs to her parents' bedroom, flinging herself onto her father's sleeping body.

'Daddy, Daddy; it's snowing and it mustn't – Granny won't be able to fetch us if it snows,' she cried.

'Wha – who – wha's the matter?' her father sat up suddenly, grabbed hold of Beth and collapsed again pulling her under the covers with him.

'Never mind, don't worry, it'll be ok,' he sank back into sleep.

Beth wriggled until she managed to escape from his hug, then she tried to wake her mother, who just turned over muttering, 'not morning yet, go back to bed.'

Beth was quite cold by this time so made her way back upstairs where she wrapped her duvet around herself and curled up on the window seat, watching the snow tumbling out of the sky. She must have dozed off because the next thing she knew Niki was leaning over her, watching the snow settling on the lawn.

'What's the time?' Beth asked. 'How soon can we phone Granny to warn her? The poor ponies will be so cold. This is going to spoil everything.'

'Don't worry, Granny won't let us down,' Niki answered. At just eleven years old Niki was used to organising her younger sisters and they usually listened to her.

2

'Come on Beth, let's wake Lolly and have a quick snowball fight before breakfast.'

The girls dressed in their oldest trousers, raced downstairs to find wellies, coats and gloves and let themselves into the back garden where the pristine snow waited for them. First they lay down on the lawn to make 'snow angels'; then made piles of snow balls which, with much whispering and giggles, they hid behind the garden wall. Then they threw snowballs at their parents' bedroom window and called to them to come down and join in the fun. Mummy opened the window and leant out to watch them.

'Oh you wretches. That nearly hit me,' she ducked as a snowball missed her by inches.

'Grrrr,' Daddy growled like a bear as he ran down the stairs.

'You don't get away with that, you little monkeys,' he shouted, leaping out of the back door.

'Aaaagh.' He was met by a barrage of snow balls as his daughters shrieked with glee.

'Got you, got you!'

Daddy raced around the garden in his bare feet, first scooping up little Lolly, then Beth, turning them upside down.

'I'll give you "Got You". Do you think you can beat The Mad Dad?' Dropping them, he chased Niki but contented himself with stuffing snow down her neck, saying, 'You're too big and heavy to be picked up, but don't think you'll get away scot free.'

Mummy called them in to breakfast, 'I don't know. Sometimes I think I have four children to look after, not just three.'

'If you're going to be rude,' Daddy said laughing as he dropped snow down her neck, 'then you should expect the worst.'

'Ouff – you rotter!' she cried, feeling wet snow seeping down her back.

Gradually calm was restored and they sat down to breakfast.

'Daddy, will Granny still be able to come and collect us with all this snow? What will we do if she can't? Will the ponies be all right? How will we have Christmas?'

Lolly, who was only just six, was worried. 'I've already written to Father Christmas to tell him I'll be at Granny's. If we can't go, he won't know where to find me.'

'We'll ring her now,' Daddy reassured them. 'I don't expect it's snowed in the south, but don't worry, you know Granny won't let a bit of snow stop her.'

So Daddy rang his mother with the children draped around him, listening carefully to every word.

'Snowing?' Granny said. 'That's ok. I'm driving the Land Rover and will bring a shovel and tow rope with me. Don't worry, I'll still be in time for the nativity play this afternoon. And I'll have blankets and flasks of soup to keep us all warm on the journey home.'

'Thanks Granny, you're the greatest. See you later. Byee,' the girls called down the phone.

Granny's practical voice had calmed the sisters and they happily dashed around cleaning teeth, collecting school bags, and making sure they were packed ready for the drive south straight after school.

Daddy gave them each a big hug and kiss before leaving for work.

'I hope your last day of term goes well, kids. Mummy and I will be down for Christmas – snow or no snow.'

Strapped into the car for the drive to school, Mummy said, 'Here's the front door key, Niki. Granny will bring you back here after school to collect your bags. Just post it back through the letter box when you leave.'

'Have a good day at school my loves. Enjoy your nativity play. Daddy and I will arrive on Christmas Eve for the rest of the holiday. Be good and look after each other.' Giving them lots of kisses, hugs and waves, Mummy left the sisters at school and drove on to her office.

The school spent the morning getting ready for their nativity play in the afternoon. The stage was set up, costumes were finished, and a general air of organised chaos prevailed.

Teachers joined the children playing in the snow before the level of excitement rose higher as children peeped from the 'wings' to see if their families had arrived. Lolly, being small, wriggled to the front and let out a shriek of glee.

'Granny's here – she's sitting with Nanny Jean – Beth, Niki, SHE'S HERE.' Niki and Beth peered around the edge of the side door and waved as their two Grannies settled themselves in seats near the front. Lolly was too excited to wait and ran down into the audience to give both her grannies big hugs.

Niki, being one of the taller children, was a Wise King with a painted moustache, a golden turban and purple cloak; Beth, along with her middle-school class-mates, was an angel in a white flowing robe with silver wings and a halo, whilst young Lolly had a 'sitting still' part as one of the sheep. As the piano began to play 'Away in a Manger' the audience quietened and the children began to file onto the stage in their costumes.

The nativity play went well; the Inn Keeper remembered most of his lines and was finally persuaded to allow Joseph and Mary into the stable; Mary didn't drop Baby Jesus; only one shepherd tripped over his long gown; the Wise Men were regal as they handed their gifts to Joseph and the animals, sheep, donkey and a cow, sat fairly still adoring the baby and his mother. The angels sang sweetly and most of them kept their halos on (although wings became a little tangled). The audience joined in singing the carols with gusto. It was a magical and moving performance of the ancient Christmas story.

All was bustle after the play finished, with madly excited children dashing around taking off their costumes, finding their school bags and wishing their friends 'Happy Christmas'.

'While the girls are busy, let's sneak outside to hide our bag of presents in your car.' Nanny Jean said to Granny Elliott. 'Then I'll say goodbye to them before you leave.'

The sisters gave Nanny Jean big hugs and kisses before climbing into the car.

'Bye bye Nanny Jean. We'll ring you on Christmas Day and see you at the end of the holidays.'

At home the sisters changed out of their uniforms while Granny managed to load their bags into the boot without the girls seeing the presents already stored in there.

'Best get a move on, girls,' Granny said. 'It's dark already and we've a long drive ahead of us.'

The countryside lay hidden under a glistening carpet of white, although it stopped snowing as they headed down the motorway, 'Pass round the sandwiches and hot soup Niki, please. Eating will help to pass the time.'

Much to Granny's relief, the excitement of the long last day of term soon caught up with the girls and they quietly dozed as they sped south for their Christmas holiday.

2

Some three hours later Granny swung the car off the motorway onto the quiet country lanes of the New Forest.

'Are you awake? It's too dark to see much but we're passing the first of the forest lawns and there may be deer grazing.'

Niki peered out of the window.

'I can't see anything except the shapes of the trees and the shadows in our headlights. They look really spooky,' she said.

'At least the snow hasn't reached this far south although it's freezing. You can see ice beginning to form on the road.' Granny showed her where water had frozen on the corners.

'Nearly there girls,' Granny announced. 'Thank goodness for the Land Rover; it really makes light work of bad weather. I'm dying for a cup of tea.'

'I can't wait to see Minou the cat and Charlie dog – oh and Grandpa of course,' said Niki.

'And Aunty Anna, and Bracken and Magic and Summer,' chorused Beth and Lolly.

'It's too dark to see the horses tonight but would you like me to wake you early to help feed them tomorrow before breakfast,' Granny teased them.

'Well, I'm not sure about that,' was Niki's considered reply.

'Yes please,' shouted Beth.

'Can I ride Magic on my own this time?' Lolly asked. 'After all I am 6 now.'

'Only 6 and 3 weeks and it's not just your age but whether your feet reach below the saddle,' Niki replied importantly. 'Of course I still have Bracken to myself; he's much too strong for Beth.'

'I love Magic very much – her dear little white face and the way she pushes her pink nose into my pocket looking for treats, but I'm quite happy to share her with you Lolly,' Beth murmured.

'Magic is white, I mean grey: Bracken is bay and big Summer is black,' chanted Lolly. 'Summer is a Rushing

Tanker horse; Bracken is a New Forest pony and Magic is Welsh.'

'Summer is a Russian Trakehner, silly,' Niki corrected her.

'Minou is black and white and so is Charlie dog,' Lolly continued, making a face at her know-it-all sister.

At long last they turned into the drive and Granny parked in front of the house. Lights were shining from the downstairs windows. The front door opened as Charlie dog and Daddy's sister Aunty Anna dashed out to welcome them. Charlie barked and bounced with excitement as the girls all hugged him while Anna helped Granny unload the car.

'The kettle's on,' Anna said to her mother. 'Luckily the snow hasn't reached us yet, but the water trough is frozen already. It looks as though we're in for a cold Christmas.'

They piled into the warm kitchen, relaxing in the heat from the Aga.

'I've made hot chocolate for you all,' Grandpa said placing mugs on the table. 'Now sit down and tell us all about school and the end of term.'

'We woke up to SNOW this morning,' Lolly started. 'We had a major snow ball fight before breakfast and Daddy stuffed snow down Mummy's neck.'

'I was very worried. We all hoped Granny could still come and fetch us,' Beth added more quietly.

'It would take more than a little snow to keep me away. Tell Grandpa about your nativity play,' Granny replied.

Niki giggled.

'I was the first Wise King which was lucky, 'cos my gift was gold. But the second Wise Man said Francesca instead of Frankincense,' she remembered. 'And the Inn Keeper didn't want to let Mary and Joseph in. When we practised, the Inn Keeper had let them in straight away so the teacher told him he had to make them wait. Then he forgot he had to let them in and Joseph got fed up and pushed past him.'

'I was an angel but my arms got tired and I nearly fell off the stage,' Beth had wanted a more active role.

'I hated being a sheep. I wanted to be a donkey and walk up to the stage, but I was too small for the costume,' Lolly had not enjoyed having to sit still for so long.

'It sounds great fun,' Grandpa exclaimed, 'I see you've grown a moustache, Niki, since we saw you last.'

'Jumping jellybeans!' Niki put her hands to her face. 'Oh, and look at Lolly's ears and whiskers.'

They all laughed loudly. In the brightly lit kitchen everyone was able to see what had been hidden in the darkness of the car; that Niki still had her Wise Man's moustache and Lolly was wearing her head-band sheep's ears and her nose was black with whiskers still painted on her checks. Niki and Lolly giggled at each other.

'And Beth's halo and wings are probably as close as she'll ever get to being an angel,' Granny teased.

'Ah well, that's over for another year. Now, have you any suggestions on what you'd like to do before Christmas?' Grandpa asked. Niki looked at her sisters.

'We need to buy presents for everyone and want to spend as much time as we can with the ponies of course. Are there any shows like last summer?'

'The Pony Club have an indoor jumping show after Christmas which I thought you might like to enter.' Anna told her nieces. 'And of course there's the Children's Meet with the New Forest Foxhounds. On Boxing Day we can watch the New Forest Point to Point. Apart from that we'll have to ride in the manège while the ground is icy.'

'What's the manège?'

'Oh, Lolly, you are silly. You know, it's where we exercise the horses when it's bad weather,' Niki said.

'I'm not silly, am I Anna? I'd just forgotten,' Lolly looked to her aunt for support.

'No, you're not silly, Lolly, it's just another word for a space with a man-made surface where we can school the horses when it's too muddy to ride on the forest,' she explained.

'Do the Foxhounds chase foxes?' asked Beth. 'I don't want to chase live animals.'

'They used to hunt foxes but not any more. These days, a rider on horseback is the "fox" and he drags a smelly rag behind him, laying a scent for the hounds to follow. It's much faster now, as there are fewer stops when hounds loose the scent and the only casualties tend to be any riders who fall off – not the foxes,' Anna reassured her nieces.

Granny said, 'I still have to do some shopping for Christmas so we can go into the market together on Saturday. There's also a Christmas Fair at the village hall with all sorts of things for sale. Father Christmas may visit too.'

Granny noticed how Lolly and Beth's faces lit up at the thought of Father Christmas, and even Niki looked interested.

'Now, come on girls, time for bed,' she added. 'The radiator is on in your room and the heat from the Aga chimney will keep you warm all night, so have your baths and we'll bring up your bags. Then just a couple of short stories and before you know it will be morning and time to see the horses.'

Granny went upstairs with them, leaving Grandpa to hide the bags of presents before sitting in the big comfy armchair in their room to read to the girls.

Cosy and with clean faces, they cuddled up under

their duvets to listen to Grandpa read their favourite stories, about the naughty puppy who could not stay out of trouble, and the mice who lived in a hedge and held an ice ball one cold winter.

'Goodnight girls; if it's still freezing tomorrow we'll have to take extra care of the horses. Who wants to get up early for feeding?' Granny asked, knowing that none of them would want to miss helping. 'I'll wake you about half past seven when it starts to get light.'

It was very cold when Granny pulled back the curtains to wake them. The girls scrambled into their jeans and warm pullovers as fast as they could and dashed downstairs to find Anna filling large water containers to take to the stables.

'Pop your wellies and coats on. Gloves and hats too. Let me help you with those, Lolly. We'll have to drive to the stables, as these are too heavy to carry. Ready everyone? OK, into the car. No, Charlie, you stay here this morning,' Anna organised her band of helpers as she and Granny lifted the full water containers into the boot. 'Oh, and Beth, I think you might be in for a surprise ... you too Lolly!'

They arrived at the yard to find not three but four heads looking out over the stable doors.

'Oh, you've got a new pony.' Beth exclaimed.

3

'Surprise, surprise, Beth! Some friends have moved
abroad for a couple of years, so we offered to look
after their daughter's pony. We thought you and Lolly
deserved one each after your success riding at the children's show last summer. Niki will still ride Bracken
and now Lolly can have Magic to herself. Beth, come
and meet Ginger.'

Beth's eyes were wide with wonder as she gazed at
the pony. 'My very own... I do love Magic, but... my
very own...'

'Niki, you give Bracken his breakfast as usual while
Lolly feeds Magic.'

Lolly proudly took Magic's bucket, hugging her with delight and talking softly to 'her' little Welsh mare.

'You're all mine now, Magic. I shall groom you and pick out your hooves all by myself.'

Anna's horse Summer kicked her stable door to encourage Granny to hurry up with her feed, while Anna let Beth into the new pony's stable.

'This is Ginger,' Anna said as Beth held out the bucket with nuts and carrots. 'She's about 13 hands high so is just right for you. Like Bracken, she's a New Forest pony. She was ridden by a girl not much older than you, and is kind and gentle. She only arrived a few days ago so it's all rather strange to her; you'll need to be quiet and patient with her until she's settled in.'

'What colour is she?'

'She's a bright chestnut.'

'Oh! She's so pretty and she has a lovely white blaze.'

Beth really felt like squealing with joy and bouncing up and down but managed to contain her excitement so she did not upset Ginger, who seemed far more interested in eating than talking to anyone. Beth gently stroked her neck and murmured quietly to her.

'We're going to have so much fun, Ginger, it's so cool you're here.'

Both Granny and Anna kept an eye on Beth and her

new pony while rugs were changed before the horses were let out into the field.

'Because Ginger doesn't know the routine yet we'll lead them all into the field instead of just letting them find their own way,' Anna said.

'Take Bracken first, Niki, then stand with him well inside the gate. Now I'll go next with Summer, Beth and Lolly follow me. Wait until Granny shuts the gate before we all take off the headcollars at the same time.'

Granny had already laid several piles of hay on the ground and Summer, who was always hungry, tucked into hers straight away but Bracken went over to Ginger for a chat and to remind her that he was the leader of this little herd. Ginger looked a bit nervous and hid behind Magic. Bracken nudged them both making them trot off round the field. Summer lifted her head from the hay and cantered after them. Everyone watched from the gate as the horses bounced around the field.

'Aren't they funny?' exclaimed Niki. 'Doesn't Bracken look like a wild stallion? I'm so glad I'm not riding him right now.'

Having persuaded the mares to canter, Bracken was tossing his head and prancing, then galloping flat out up the field, head high, his black mane and tail flowing in the wind. Magic and Summer were used to him playing and were quite happy to gallop after him.

Ginger was more cautious, but she was soon caught up in the excitement and joined in. They raced around the field, skidding to a halt as they reached the fences, then galloped off again, bucking and swerving and teasing each other until they slowed down, puffing, and settled to eat their hay.

'That's good; they needed to stretch their legs after a night in the stable. Luckily none of them is bad tempered or likely to kick so Ginger will be quite safe,' Anna said.

'You're going to have so much fun this holiday,' Granny said, giving Beth a quick hug. 'Now I'll go and get breakfast ready while you muck out the stables.'

It was a very lively family who sat around the kitchen table some time later. Lolly was thrilled that she didn't have to share Magic any more. Niki was content to keep her beloved Bracken, and Beth was so excited she found it hard to sit still.

'I can't wait to get to know Ginger; can I ride her this morning?' she asked.

'The ground is thawing so we'll ride in the field a bit later,' Anna decided, much to Beth's delight.

'We'll clear away breakfast before going back to the stables. Come on Charlie dog; you can come with us this time.' Niki let Charlie hold his lead in his mouth.

The ponies had finished their hay and were dozing behind the hedge. They were quite happy to be caught as they found cold weather very boring. Anna led in Summer, making sure the two smaller mares followed Bracken through the gate.

'Niki, will you check on Lolly picking out Magic's hooves;, and she might need help brushing where the tack touches. I'll keep an eye on Beth and Ginger.'

Lolly wasn't pleased to have her big sister bossing her around.

'I can do it by myself,' she said, tossing her head at Niki. 'You stay outside. I know what to do.'

'Aunty Anna told me to help,' Niki grumbled, retreating to groom Bracken but sensibly watching quietly.

Beth talked to Ginger while she was grooming her.

'I hope you'll be happy in your new home, Ginger,' she said. 'I'll love you just as much as your other little girl did. We'll have so much fun, jumping and riding on the forest. Magic and Bracken are really sweet and will look after you too.'

Ginger seemed to listen, standing quietly and flicking her ears in response to the girl's voice.

'Are you lot ready?' Anna called. 'Cold weather can make them lively so you may have to hang on tightly. I'll give you a leg up Beth, and you to, Lolly. Niki you'd better take Bracken in first, in case he bombs off; we don't want them all going do-lally at the same time.'

Anna checked their girths were tight and their hats done up before the girls mounted, holding onto Magic and Ginger as Bracken pushed through the gate frisk-ily.

'Keep his head up so he can't buck,' she called out to Niki as, full of beans, Bracken broke into a fast trot.

'Oh, jumping jellybeans, I'd forgotten how strong he can be,' squealed Niki as he took off across the field. 'Steady boy, calm down.'

When Anna was sure Bracken had worked the tickle out of his toes she let go of Ginger.

'Ask her to walk on, Beth. She might be a little reluct-ant but I'm sure she'll soon gain confidence.' Anna gave the pony a light pat on the rump and Ginger picked her way daintily through the muddy gateway.

Always the big sister, Niki rode alongside her sister to give her confidence, although Bracken's head toss-ing and jogging sideways had the opposite effect.

'Go away Niki. Let me ride around on my own,' Beth pleaded.

'Can I go too now please? I don't need to be on the lead rein in the field,' Lolly said, certain she could manage Magic on her own. Anna led her into the field and let go of the little pony who tucked her chin into her chest and trotted rapidly across the field to join the others. Lolly hadn't been expecting such a fast trot and bumped around, nearly falling out of the saddle, but she managed to hang on and thankfully the pony stopped once she had reached her friends.

'Phew. That was bumpy. Cantering is more comfy,' Lolly exclaimed.

'Ride around the arena markers, keeping plenty of room between you all,' Anna instructed. 'I want you to walk once round, then trot all the way around before turning and going the other way. When the ponies have calmed down and you're happy, you can canter on one at a time, starting with Niki.'

Bracken was still full of bounce and Niki struggled to stay in the saddle as he bucked and pranced. She had to overtake the others several times before he settled.

Beth wasn't sure how Ginger would react once she was in front but the little pony behaved perfectly.

'I expect she's being extra good because she's in a new place. You may find she perks up a bit as you get to know each other,' Anna advised.

Magic didn't like being left behind, especially with Bracken crowding up behind her, and cantered off after Ginger, with Lolly laughing too much to stop her.

'Stop laughing Lolly,' Anna said strictly. 'You mustn't let her get away with being naughty otherwise she'll keep misbehaving and you won't like it when you're out on the forest.' At last Anna was satisfied that the girls and their ponies were under control and warmed up.

Back in the yard, Niki helped her younger sisters

to untack their ponies and lift the saddles onto their racks in the tack room, while Anna mounted Summer for a quick work out in the field. The girls sat on the gate and watched their aunt put Summer through her paces; flicking her hooves out in front in trot, cantering sideways across the marked arena ('that's called half pass I think,' muttered Niki), then practising 'flying changes'.

'Gosh, Summer's dancing,' exclaimed Lolly. 'All she needs is music.'

'We have a dressage to music competition coming up and I need to put together a CD of suitable music. Would you like to help me?' Anna asked as she removed Summer's saddle and bridle. 'I need some slow marching music for the walk, then a faster beat for the trot, and the canter and flying changes need light floaty music.'

'We could do a mixture of Christmas Carols,' Beth thought aloud. 'Something gentle like Away in a Manger for the walking, then Hark the Herald Angels Sing with the chorus of Alleluia for the canter and changes.'

'Yes and While Shepherds Washed Their Socks By Night,' Lolly giggled. She had only just learnt the words.

'Silly – it's the rhythm we need, not the words,' Niki

scoffed. 'But actually that is quite a good one for trot. Good King Wenceslas has a strong beat too.'

'You could finish with Silent Night,' added Beth who had loved singing the carols at school.

'What a good idea. I know, we'll ask Granny to play the piano and you can sing the carols while I record it onto my lap top. Then we can play it back while I work out a routine on Summer to fit the music.' Anna was delighted to think that her dressage would be both unique and seasonal.

'Right. Horses rugged and ready to go back into the field until supper? Then let's head indoors for some hot chocolate and toasted feet in front of the Aga.' So saying, Anna grabbed Lolly's hand and ran back across the little bridge towards the house. Niki and Beth followed laughing and skipping.

4

'We must go and see Mervyn and Mrs Mavis and Mrs Ambridge to wish them a happy Christmas,' Niki said at lunch.

'I hope they've got us pressies,' Lolly exclaimed.

'You shouldn't think like that,' Beth scolded her young sister. 'We go to see them 'cos we love them,' she added, primly.

'That's a good idea, Niki. The ponies will be happy in the field until tea time and you can ride again tomorrow. If you see Mervyn you might ask if he'll check Ginger's shoes as I don't know when she was last shod,' Anna said.

The girls loved visiting the friendly blacksmith.

With Charlie dog bouncing happily beside them, they squeezed through the hedge and skipped along the drive to the forge, where for the first time ever its door was firmly shut.

'Oh, p'rhaps he's not here,' Beth was disappointed.

'Mervyn. Mervyn. Let us in,' Lolly shouted at the top of her voice, banging on the door with all her might.

'Ho, what's all this noise then?' The door swung open and there stood Mervyn, with a cup of something hot steaming in his hand. 'I was just taking 40 winks beside the fire but come in, come in, my dears, and find somewhere to sit. Would you like a hot drink?'

As the girls sat on old sacks and upturned logs, Mervyn picked a red hot poker out of the furnace and thrust it into mugs of water, where it sizzled, sending spirals of steam into the air. Then he stirred drinking chocolate into the mugs, handing them round before sitting back in his old rocking chair with its tattered cushion. While the girls watched wide eyed he took a leather flask from a shelf and poured a liquid into his own mug, saying, 'A little something even warmer to keep my old bones moving sweetly.'

Mervyn took a sip of his drink, and the girls cautiously sipped theirs. Beth was worried that the poker might have left bits in it, but apart from a slightly scorched taste, the warming drink was very welcome.

'Now, what can I do for you young ladies?' Mervyn asked.

'We – that is, Beth – that is Anna – has a new pony,' Niki started importantly.

'So Magic is all mine now,' Lolly added.

'Her name is Ginger and she's very sweet. Anna wants to know if you'll check her feet as we don't know how old her shoes are,' Beth butted in quickly; as Ginger was her pony, she decided she should do the asking.

'There now, that's grand,' Mervyn twinkled at them. 'I did wonder last summer how long you two could keep sharing. You bring her along any old time. I don't go out visiting in this weather so I'll be here. Might be best to bring the other little 'un along to keep her company, first time, like.'

'What a good idea. Yes, we'll do that. Perhaps tomorrow after breakfast so I'll still have time to ride?' Beth agreed quickly, before her bossy sisters could butt in.

The heat from the furnace made the forge very comfortable and the girls relaxed, chatting to the blacksmith and examining the delicate ornaments he had fashioned from iron.

'This here's a lamp stand I made for a lady in the village, and here are some door latches and handles for the young chap who's bought a thatched cottage just upalong.'

'Oh how sweet, they're shaped like mouse and cat tails,' Beth exclaimed.

'Have you seen the gates I made for your Grandpa?' Mervyn asked, raising his bushy eyebrows.

'No, it was dark when we arrived last night but we'll go and inspect them straight away,' Niki answered.

'Did you put our names on them?' Lolly remembered he had promised to do this during their summer visit.

'Aye, I did that. Good thing you've got short names. Didn't take long,' he replied.

'Bye Mervyn, see you tomorrow,' the girls pulled on their coats before heading out into the cold and back through the hedge.

'Let's have a race down the drive and look at the gates to wake ourselves up, then we can go and say hello to Mrs A and Mrs Mavis,' Niki was back in charge and Lolly yelled;

'Ready, Teddy, GO.' Although they ran as fast as they could, Charlie was faster and they arrived laughing and breathless to look at the new gates.

'Look, here's my name, and there's yours, Lolly, near the bottom.'

Lolly traced her name with her finger, as they exclaimed at the clever decorations.

'Here's a little bird – his chest is all puffed up, I bet he's a robin.'

'Oh look, there's a bunch of grapes.'

'Here's a rabbit looking out from behind this clump of grass.'

'Your name is high up Niki, and you have a snail crawling across the N.'

'The o in my name is an animal – I think it's a ladybird,' Lolly said in wonder.

'What have you got Beth? What has he given you?'

'A dear little mouse,' Beth replied happily. 'We must think of a way to thank Mervyn, he's taken so much trouble.'

'We'll look for something at the Christmas fair with Granny,' Niki said. 'We've brought plenty of pocket money so we'll find him something really special. Now, come on, off to see Mrs Ambridge and Mrs Mavis.'

'I wonder if they'll have some biscuits or a piece of Christmas cake,' said Lolly who was always ready for a little something to eat.

The ladies lived across the lawn from Granny and Grandpa, in two cottages which had been knocked into one, and were covered with climbing roses in the summer.

The windows were brightly lit with fairy lights sparkling on a small Christmas tree. They hardly had time to knock before the door was flung open.

'We wondered when you would call – look, even Minou got here first for her saucer of warm milk.' So saying the two ladies, one short and round and the other tall and thin, bustled around, sitting the girls down at the scrubbed kitchen table and offering drinks and chocolate cake, while Charlie made himself comfortable under the table, where he could catch any crumbs that came his way.

'Oh goody. My favourite,' Lolly tucked in fast and soon had chocolate smeared all round her face.

'Where are your manners, child?' exclaimed Niki in her mother's voice. 'Go and wash your hands at once.'

'I'm sorry. It's so delicious,' Lolly sprayed crumbs as she tried to speak with her mouth full.

'Never mind just this once, dear. After all it is Christmas and we're so pleased to see you,' Mrs Mavis said calmly.

'But you'd better wash your face before your Gran sees you,' Mrs Ambridge added.

When all the gossip, and most especially the news about Beth's new pony, had been exchanged, Niki stood up.

'We have to go now. It's time to feed the ponies and help Anna put them to bed. Thank you for a lovely tea and we'll see you again soon.'

Beth scooped up the sleeping Minou and Lolly held Charlie's collar as the girls waved goodbye, heading back to Granny's house.

5

The next morning Anna found Beth and Niki already in the kitchen, dressed and ready to feed the ponies.

'Gosh, you're early birds. What brought this on?' she exclaimed.

'I wanted to give Ginger her bucket so she gets to know me quickly, and Niki heard me,' Beth explained.

'Well, it's still dark so I think we've time for a hot drink first. Then we need to fill the water containers as it froze again overnight.'

'What shall we do today? Can we ride or is the ground too hard?' Niki asked, licking chocolate froth from her lips.

'I sometimes take Summer to my friend Emma's

manège down the road rather than ride in the field. I'll give her a ring after breakfast and see if we can use it this morning. You lot need to practise your jumping for the Christmas show; after all you haven't ridden since half term and we only have a week to prepare.'

Beth gave Ginger lots of hugs and pats, exclaiming delightedly. 'Did you hear her? She whinnied to me. She's getting to know me already.'

Anna rather thought the whinny might have been for the bucket of nuts, but didn't spoil Beth's pleasure by saying anything.

It didn't take long to feed the ponies, put on their outdoor rugs and turn them out in the field where they kicked up their heels and had a quick chase around before settling down to the serious business of eating the hay which Niki and Beth had laid out in piles, spaced well apart so that the horses didn't feel crowded.

'Come on girls. We need to muck out the stables before breakfast. I'll do Magic's as Lolly isn't here.'

'Mucking out is very warming, my fingers are tingling but I still can't feel my toes,' Niki said as she pushed the full wheelbarrow to the muck heap.

'The best thing about winter is Granny's Aga,' Beth said and the others agreed, working quickly so they could return to the kitchen.

They kicked off their wellies in the outer porch,

stuffing gloves into coat pockets, and flung open the kitchen door to dash across to the Aga and warm their toes.

'Shut that door,' bellowed Grandpa, rustling his newspaper and making comic faces at the girls.

'Porridge everyone?' Granny asked. 'Brown sugar or syrup?' as she handed round steaming bowls.

'How many helpings have you had Lolly? You'll burst if you have any more,' she added.

'But my bowl is very small, Granny. And my tummy isn't full yet.'

Anna had a text back from her friend Emma.

'We can have the school from eleven o'clock every day this week. We'll pop into Mervyn's forge to check Ginger's hooves on our way, which will be good as she'll have company for her first visit. So let's clear the table for Granny and then you'd better change into your johds and riding boots.'

The three girls thundered up the stairs to change. Their bedroom was above the kitchen and the warmth from the Aga below kept it extra cosy. Niki used to share the big double bed with Beth while Lolly had the 'cot bed'. This year Granny had bought a single bed for Niki and now Lolly shared the big bed with Beth. Niki proudly made her bed with its new pony duvet cover, while Beth and Lolly just patted theirs and bounced around while they changed into their riding clothes.

'I can't hardly walk I have so many clothes on,' Lolly said waddling like a penguin. 'How will I get on Magic?'

'Silly girl. You don't need all those pullovers as you'll have your coat on and hat and gloves. You'll warm up riding too,' Niki dragged Lolly's extra pullovers off her little sister.

'There, that's better isn't it. Come on, I can hear Charlie barking for us.'

For once the ponies were easy to catch; they'd finished their hay and there wasn't much grass to interest them.

Anna trusted Niki to groom and tack up Bracken on her own, while she kept an eye on the younger girls. Lolly had to stand on an upturned bucket to reach Magic's back.

'Put on these fluorescent tabards so car drivers can see us. Ready everyone? Niki you'd better follow Beth while I have Lolly with me.'

Anna gave Lolly a leg up before mounting Summer herself.

'Will you open the gate please Niki, but there's no need to shut it behind us. Once we reach the road I'll put you on the lead rein, Lolly. Charlie, heel. Let's go,' Anna organised her cavalcade and they walked down the drive until they reached Mervyn's forge.

'Morning Miss Anna; morning girls. My, you do look

neat and dandy. Is this the new pony?' Mervyn ran his hand down Ginger's neck and patted her before stooping down to pick up a front foot and then a back one. 'Hmm. Well, her feet are good but she'll need road nails if this weather continues. Call back after your ride, I'll just hammer a couple in without disturbing her shoes.'

'Thanks Mervyn; that'll be great. See you later. Bye.'

They rode down the quiet country lane in single file.

Once Anna was sure everyone was comfortable she called 'Trot on,' and put Summer into a slow trot so that Magic could keep up. Bracken was not happy at the back and kept tossing his head but Niki sat up tall and told him to 'whoa' until at last he settled quietly behind Ginger.

Anna slowed to a walk as they arrived at her friend's yard. Horses' heads appeared at stable doors, neighing a greeting to the newcomers. A girl pushing a wheelbarrow shouted a greeting.

'Hi everyone. The school is all yours. If you want I can come and help with the jumps after I've finished mucking out.'

'Great, thanks. Girls, this is Emma – you may remember her from last summer.'

'Oh yes, how's Fudge?' Lolly wanted to know about the little Shetland she had ridden. 'I liked riding Fudge but Magic's all mine now.'

'Fudge is fine, she's teaching my daughter to ride these days. Is this the new pony for Beth? She looks a steady sort. What a stroke of luck being offered her.' Emma smiled, patting Ginger who stood quietly while Summer and Bracken jiggled around impatiently.

'Yes, Ginger has good manners, just right for Beth. The girls' riding at the summer show impressed the Pony Club District Commissioner so much she put in a good word for us.'

'Now, you girls ride single file on the inside track and I'll keep Summer close to the fence as she's likely to bounce. Trot a couple of times around the school, then cross over the diagonal and trot the other way. Then, one at a time, the lead pony canters round to the back of the file, just as you did yesterday. That should warm up everyone so the ponies will be ready to do some jumping.'

Beth was a little nervous once she was 'lead' rider, but again Ginger behaved perfectly and she soon relaxed. The pony liked having a gentle rider and responded well to Beth's light hands. Bracken, however, was showing off, tossing his head and side stepping. When Niki asked him to canter he sprang into the air, nearly unseating her, and charged off at a fast pace.

'Whoa. Steady up you horror,' Niki shouted, sitting up and pulling hard on the reins as they approached

Magic a bit too fast. Just in time, Niki remembered how to stop him by turning a circle and at last she had him back under control.

'He's full of himself this morning,' her face was bright pink but laughing, too. 'He's a naughty pony, but I'm not scared of him any more.'

'I'm glad Ginger is quieter, I only have to think "stop" and she does,' Beth said, patting the pony's neck.

'Look at me. I'm cantering all by myself,' Lolly shouted, grinning widely as Magic cantered back to her friends.

'It's good you haven't forgotten how to ride. Now let's see how you manage some jumps,' Anna said, pleased.

Anna left Summer 'tied up loose' with her reins tucked under her stirrup leathers so she wouldn't tread on them, and helped Emma put out some jumps. Bracken was still over excited; he hated schooling but loved jumping and cantered straight over the poles almost before Niki was ready.

'You need to take charge, Niki, otherwise when the jumps are bigger you'll get into all sorts of trouble. Now, your turn Beth; canter on and give her plenty of time to see the jumps. Oh, well done. She popped those nicely. Do you want to be led Lolly?'

'No. I can do it myself,' Lolly said stoutly, sitting

down in the saddle as Magic cantered towards the first jump. Magic took off over the jump and Lolly was jerked forward.

'Oh, I forgot to lean forward. Can I try again,' she called.

'You all need to go again before we raise the jumps.'

The girls jumped several more times until Anna was satisfied they were in control, then she raised the poles.

'Once more at this height in each direction, and Niki, I want to see you in charge of that nutter you're riding,' Anna called.

Bracken still thought these jumps were too small and rushed them, but Ginger popped over them like an angel. Lolly kicked Magic into canter and remembered to lean forward so she was not pulled out of the saddle.

'Magic is easier to ride in here, where there's no grass for her to eat,' she said as she slowed the pony to walk again.

'Well done everyone. Those jumps are about 2 feet high – or 60 centimetres – which is probably what you'll jump at the show, Lolly. We'll raise them for you two though, as I expect your class will start at 70 cms and possibly rise to 80cms in a jump off.'

Lolly was disappointed not to jump again but cheered up when Anna said she could jump higher tomorrow. Beth was delighted that Ginger was such a steady pony, as Bracken was still pulling hard and Niki's arms were tired by the time Anna said they'd done enough.

'Are you going to jump Summer?' Emma asked. 'If someone holds Bracken, Niki can help me to raise the jumps for Anna.'

'Gosh those are really big.' Beth gasped as Emma altered the poles. 'How high is that?'

'I've started her at 100cm but if they're any lower she hardly even sees them.'

Summer, like Bracken, was excited by the thought of jumping and Anna had to say 'Wait, wait, wait...' as they approached the first obstacle. Summer made an enormous leap and landed very close to the second jump. She then had to take off after one short stride and had to really stretch for the third jump.

'Serves you right, you silly horse. Next time just listen to me instead of thinking you know best,' Anna told her.

This time, Summer settled and waited for Anna to tell her when to take off.

'Much better. You'll have to listen this time, too, as the jumps are much higher.'

By the time they had cleared 110 cms Anna decided it was time they went home and, with much cheerful waving and thanks to Emma for her help, they set off.

'Niki, if you stay with Beth while Ginger has the road nails put in, I'll ride on to the stables with Lolly, then you can ride back together,' Anna said when they reached Mervyn's forge.

The two girls grinned, feeling very proud at being allowed to ride home alone.

Father Christmas
Gone to feed the Reindeer

6

'It's the Christmas fair this afternoon in the village. Who wants to come with me?' Granny asked as they sat over warming bowls of tomato soup for a late lunch.

'Me, me, me,' the girls all shouted.

'We need to buy presents for loads of people.'

'I've been saving my pocket money all term.'

'I want to see Father Christmas.'

'I think I'll come too. I still have some gifts to buy,' Anna added.

'I shall stay here and help Charlie and Minou keep an eye on the fire,' Grandpa said.

With Niki organising her sisters into changing out

of their riding clothes and finding their purses, they were soon ready.

'We'll put our wellies and riding coats in the car so we can feed the horses on the way home,' Anna decided.

'Everyone in? Off we go.' The girls waved as Charlie watched sadly from the window.

'He hates being left behind. We'll have to give him extra cuddles tonight,' Beth said.

'Can you imagine the chaos his long swishy tail would bring to the stalls,' Anna said laughing. The sisters giggled at the thought.

'He had the most beautiful tail in the Dog with the Waggiest Tail class last year,' Lolly remembered, 'but we do have to 'member not to put mugs low down when he's around.'

'Here we are, everyone out,' so saying Granny led the way into the already crowded hall.

'We need to find something for Mervyn, Mrs A and Mrs Mavis, Emma for letting us ride at her yard, and of course for Mummy and Dad, Granny, Grandpa and Aunty Anna.' Niki counted on her fingers.

'Don't forget the ponies and Charlie dog and Minou,' Lolly was bouncing up and down with excitement.

'Gosh, that is a lot of presents. I hope we've enough money,' Beth was worried.

'And a visit to Father Christmas,' Lolly added, seeing

a notice saying, 'Gone to feed the Reindeer. Back Later. Signed, Santa.'

'Give me your money so we know how much we have to spend. Then we'll start at this end and work our way round,' Niki said bossily, but her sisters didn't mind as she usually had good ideas. Lolly, being small, wriggled through the crowd to the front of the first stall, where home made soft toys, knitted gloves, hat and scarf sets, egg cosies and embroidered ornaments were displayed.

'Mrs Ambridge and Mrs Mavis might find those tea cosies useful, but the knitted gloves are no good for Mervyn – they would burn.'

'Look at that pretty cloth horse with the embroidered saddle and bridle and bright shiny eyes. Do you think Emma or Aunty Anna would like that?'

'Excuse me,' Niki asked the stall holder. 'How much is the embroidered horse?'

'How much is it?' Beth whispered, tugging Niki's sleeve.

'She said £5 for the large one but they have smaller ones at £2.50. The cosies are £1 each.'

'Let's buy those tea cosies, one green and one blue, for the two ladies, and the smaller horse for Emma. We can come back for a fancy purse or the larger horse later if we have some money left over.'

The next stall specialised in hand painted china;

mugs, plates, bowls and tiles had pictures of cats, dogs or boats on them. The girls decided they couldn't afford much there so moved on to the next table which had pieces of wood carved into animals of the forest, or just rubbed down into fantastic shapes. There was a stall with hand made jewellery and another with Christmas decorations. They lingered longingly in front of the second hand toys and jigsaws, then they noticed a display of leather items.

'How about this wallet for Grandpa, and here's a belt for Mervyn and a posh mobile phone holder for Dad,' Niki suggested.

'Mmm, I like the phone holder and belt but there was a cute carved owl on the wood stall which Grandpa would love,' Beth said.

On the bric-a-brac stall they found a dainty saucer for Minou's milk and a metal bowl for Charlie dog's supper. There was a long string of shiny stones with a matching brooch that they thought Granny would like, and a dainty butterfly necklace for Mummy.

Niki stowed their purchases in her rucksack saying, 'We still need to find something for Aunty Anna and the horses.'

Lolly let out a squeal and dashed across the hall with her sisters following. She had seen just the thing for Anna.

'Look,' she said pointing to a china horse head. 'It's

got a blaze just like Summer. Anna can hang it on her bedroom wall.'

'That's everyone sorted and we've still got £4 each to spend,' Niki said handing the money back to Beth and Lolly. 'Let's split up now,' she added, intending to find a present for each of her sisters.

Dreamy Beth didn't know where to go first but Lolly made straight for the grotto to find out when Father Christmas would be back. The 'elf' in charge told her he should arrive soon so Lolly sat down.

'I need to be first 'cos we have to feed the ponies before it gets dark,' she said firmly.

Beth remembered she had seen some horsey books on the second hand book stall and bought two for Niki, as well as a book mark made from pressed flowers. Then she went back to the first stall where she had noticed a purse with a zip that she knew Lolly would love. She desperately wanted the embroidered horse but knew she mustn't spend money on herself.

Niki knew that Beth had loved the fancy horse but didn't have enough money left, so she found Granny and asked if they could buy it together.

'What a good idea, I was wondering what to get her,' Granny said and they chose the biggest, pinkest one there.

'What about you, Niki? What would you like, and have you any ideas for Lolly?'

'I haven't really seen anything for me, but Lolly liked a jigsaw of two horses pulling a plough which should keep her quiet for a bit.'

Suddenly there was urgent shushing around the hall and as people quietened and stopped talking, faint bells could be heard coming closer and louder.

'It's Father Christmas; he's coming at last,' Lolly shouted, making everyone laugh. Sure enough the doors swung open and a very jolly Santa was blown in on a gust of cold air.

'Ho ho ho,' he said, lowering his sack to the floor. 'Who's first?' and Lolly bounced up to him.

'Me. I am. My pony needs her supper soon and I've been waiting for AGES,' she announced.

'Well then, let me sit down and see what I can find for you,' Father Christmas delved into his sack. He found what he was looking for and handed a present to Lolly who was trembling with excitement.

'Here it be, me dear,' he rumbled and watched as she tore open the paper.

'Oh, look Granny, a horseshoe nail necklace. How clever of Father Christmas to know I have a pony.'

As instructed by Granny, Beth and Niki sheepishly joined the queue of younger children. Father Christmas winked at them as he handed them similar packages. They whispered 'thank you very much Father

Christmas,' as they hugged him, delighted with their horseshoe nail necklaces.

'Look, Beth, your's is shaped like a B, and mine is an L and Niki has a N. Wow, isn't Father Christmas clever,' Lolly insisted on wearing hers straight away.

'Have you bought everything you want? We'd better find Anna and go, it's time for evening stables.'

7

Another frosty day meant they had to ride in the manège rather than on the forest.

'At least I can try my dressage to music, now we've put the carols on my IPod,' Anna said as they tacked up the ponies.

As usual they rode together around the arena, with Anna reminding them to sit up straight in the saddle, keep their hands soft and their legs still, so the ponies would want to be obedient. Then Emma suggested they put the ponies into a couple of empty stables so that Anna and Summer could practise by themselves.

Niki set the music at full volume and Anna began

to run through the movements she had planned. To begin with, Niki had to keep stopping and restarting the music while Anna worked out how many strides were needed to cross the school, then she would try again, keeping in time to the rhythm. Summer loved music and looked as though she was nodding her head in time to the beat.

'Oh, Anna's making it look as if Summer's dancing,' Beth sighed. 'If only I could do that on Ginger.'

'Those are flying changes,' Niki said knowledgeably as Anna asked Summer to change legs every other stride.

'I like the bit where she gallops down the centre of the school,' Lolly said stoutly.

Niki was too busy writing down the changes Anna was making to say much.

'I hope there's time to jump before we leave,' was her only comment.

'OK girls. I think Summer deserves a rest now, so I'll pop her into a stable and we'll put out the jumps. Niki, you need to really take control this time and not let Bracken run away with you. Beth, Ginger is so obedient you only have to point her in the right direction so today I want to see you asking her to jump from an angle rather than straight, and also change her speed around the course.'

'What do I need to do on my Magic?' Lolly asked as her older sisters set off.

'I want you to watch and tell me what you think they're doing right or not, how they are sitting in the saddle, if their reins are too long or short. Then you can try to do it better on Magic,' Anna answered.

'Well, first off,' Lolly said smugly, 'they haven't shortened their stirrups.'

'Quite right,' Anna laughed. 'Did you hear that girls? Shorten your stirrup leathers a couple of holes each.'

Niki went around the set of jumps first, taking the corners wide to make Bracken slow down, with Anna calling out:

'Sit up, make him wait for the jump to come to him. Keep your hands down, look past the jump. Now look towards the next jump so he turns without needing you to pull his mouth. Well done, that's the way.'

It seemed to take Bracken a long time to settle down and stop pulling, but at last Niki was able to keep him straight and complete the course calmly.

Beth had the opposite problem; trying to encourage Ginger to lengthen her stride, so Anna told her to cut her corners and take the jumps, which were still quite low, at odd angles. Ginger seemed surprised at being asked to go faster but soon began to enjoy herself.

'My turn. My turn now,' Lolly bounced up and down, fed up with watching the others.

'Ok, off you go. Remember to give with your hands as you go over the jumps so you don't jab Magic in the mouth. Keep your legs still, don't flap,' Anna called.

Then she raised the jumps.

'Summer much prefers jumping to flat work, I'll just let her have a quick round as she's been so good,' she said.

'No kidding. She should have been named Whizz,' the girls laughed as Summer flew over the jumps, with Anna encouraging her to cut corners, shorten her stride over the double and then lengthen again. They finished with a flying lap around the arena before pulling up at the gate, with Summer snorting and cracking her nostrils.

'Home now and let's hope the ground is soft enough for us to ride on the forest tomorrow,' Anna said as they clattered out of the yard, waving to Emma.

'Have you any plans for this afternoon?' Grandpa asked over lunch. 'Nothing special? Would you like to come with me to choose the Christmas tree?'

'Can we have a big one please, Grandpa? Ours at home is always small 'cos there isn't much room,' Beth asked, hopefully.

'Oh, yes please. We could have a real whopper here,' Niki added.

'We'll have to tie it onto the roof rack if it's going to

be that big. I'd better take some rope with us.' Grandpa looked at their excited faces.

'Once we've put up the tree it'll really feel like Christmas,' Niki declared.

'Where would you like it? In the sitting room or in the kitchen?' Grandpa asked.

'Oh in here. We never sit next door as it's so cosy by the Aga,' Beth said, looking around.

'If we put it over by the stairs, it could be really huge and not in our way at all,' Niki said thoughtfully.

'Right, here's a tape measure. You girls find out how tall and wide it can be, while I fetch Granny's Land Rover and find some rope.'

Niki took charge, as usual.

'Lolly, move Charlie's bed over. Beth, shove that chair to one side and then hold the bottom of the tape while I go up the stairs to measure.'

The girls quickly made a space and Niki hung over the banisters, holding the tape all the way up to the ceiling.

'I make that – er – 2500 centimetres, two and a half metres.'

'Hmmph,' said Grandpa, coming back into the room with a coil of rope, 'and how much is that in feet and inches? I still can't fathom the metric stuff. It's written on the other side of the tape, Niki.'

55

'Err, oh, it's – 8 feet 2 inches, Grandpa.' He nodded as he disappeared out of the door.

'Now for the width,' she bounded down the stairs and they carefully measured from the wall out into the room.

'There's got to be room to put all the presents round,' Lolly said.

'Perhaps 125 centimetres or 4 feet will be about right then.'

'Don't forget to leave enough room for the star on the top,' Beth reminded her sister.

'Coo, you lot are so fussy,' humphed Niki. 'All right; we'll ask Grandpa for a tree just under 8 feet and between 4 and 5 feet fat at the bottom.'

'Quick, coats and boots on, he's waiting,' Lolly shouted as she heard a toot from the car horn.

'Where are we going?' Niki asked as Grandpa drove up a New Forest track. 'We always buy ours from a shop.'

'The Forestry Commission cuts trees and sell them in the forest rather than a town. It can be muddy so it's a good thing you're wearing your wellies. Look, here we are.'

He swung into a space in the muddy car park and the girls dashed ahead of him towards the huge piles of trees which were being inspected by crowds of people. Niki grabbed a tree.

'How about this one?'

'Better measure it. They look smaller when they're out in the open,' Grandpa advised her.

'Trust you, Niki. It's over 13 feet,' Beth giggled as she rewound the tape measure.

'Well, you choose, then,' Niki walked off in a huff.

They looked at lots of trees, some had long branches too widely spaced, some didn't have a 'good' side, some didn't have branches to the top, and some had been cut off too short at the bottom so there wouldn't be enough trunk to put in a bucket.

The light was beginning to fade and Lolly was cold and tired. Her nose was runny too.

'How about this one?' she said, just grabbing the tree nearest to her.

'Oh, oh yes, that looks a likely one,' Grandpa looked it over. 'Right height, not too wide, good branches, good length of trunk to plant in the bucket, yes I like it. What do you think girls?'

'The branches are nice and thick.'

'And there are lots of them 'cos we've got loads of decorations.'

With a sigh of relief Grandpa paid and they struggled across the car park with it. Niki had to stand up on the running board to help Grandpa lift it onto the roof rack of the Land Rover, and then they covered it with a rug to protect the needles before tying it down.

'Phew. That's a good job done. It can stay in the garage tonight and I'll pot it in the morning. Now home for hot chocolate and a biscuit,' Grandpa said.

'And then it'll be time to feed the ponies and give them good night kisses,' Beth replied happily.

8

Thankfully the next day was not quite so cold and the three girls and their aunt rode to the forest in high spirits, well wrapped up against the chilly wind. The horses were just as pleased to hack out rather than going around an arena and fairly skipped along, skittering and shying at anything that moved.

'Oh, heavens, stop that Bracken,' yelped Niki as he jumped an invisible gorse bush.

'Even Ginger has the wind under her tail,' Beth laughed as her gentle pony hopped over a twig.

Lolly, back on the lead rein but hoping to be allowed off soon, made sure that Magic kept up with Summer.

'Can I ride on my own please Anna. Magic has to jog to stay with Summer and is bouncing me about lots.'

'Sorry, pet, but I'm afraid she'll dash off after Bracken when we reach the green. But I'll tell you what, as Ginger is so quiet, perhaps Beth will hold your rein.'

'Heavens, must I? Can I? Well, I'll give it a go,' Beth was nervous but willing to try.

By the time they reached the green, both Bracken and Summer were dancing sideways, longing to have a gallop. Ginger's ears were pricked but she stood quietly; Magic seemed happy to stay with her.

Anna called to Niki, 'You go first and I'll catch you up. Start turning him before the end of the green and come back to the others.'

Almost before she had finished speaking, Bracken had bounded forward and, with Niki leaning over his neck, was racing across the open space. Summer was desperate to gallop too and nearly dragged the reins out of Anna's hands before she was allowed to follow. Anna crouched low as they rapidly caught up smaller Bracken, who put on a spurt as he heard them coming up behind him.

'All right?' Anna asked as she sped by.

'Oh yes,' gasped Niki, eyes watering in the cold air.

The horses had no intention of slowing down yet and were well into their second circuit of the green before their riders sat up and eased them down into a canter. Even the riders were puffing as they walked back to the younger girls.

'No need to ask if you want a gallop,' Anna said as Lolly bounced up and down impatiently. 'I'll unclip the lead rein so you can go at your own speed. Remember to turn well before you reach the gorse bushes at the end of the green.'

'Come on Magic, come on Beth,' Lolly kicked Magic who went straight into canter, followed by Ginger. The two girls were side by side but Lolly wanted to go faster and leant forward urging her pony to race.

Ginger seemed quite content to follow closely until Beth, gaining confidence, kicked her on, laughing at Lolly's cross face when they overtook her.

Everyone was tingling and warm now and with the ponies calmer Anna led them along narrow paths through the gorse bushes, jumping any that were suitable, and before the girls knew it, they had ridden in a large circle and were on their way home.

'Can't we stay out longer?' Niki asked.

'No, best not. Look at Lolly's face – it's scarlet with cold, Beth is beginning to hunch her shoulders and I can't feel my feet. Come on, brisk trot until we reach the road then walk in single file, and don't forget to thank any drivers for slowing down as they pass.'

Granny had been baking and they were greeted with the delicious smell of fresh crusty bread.

'Oh, yummy, and home made vegetable soup. Can we dunk please?' Beth asked as she warmed herself in front of the Aga.

'Phew, your feet are beginning to steam,' Niki held her nose. 'Oh, look, Grandpa has brought the tree in. It fits that space perfectly.'

'I'm hoping you'll help me decorate the house and tree this afternoon,' Granny said. 'I've brought all the ornaments down from the loft for you.'

'Can we decorate the stables please Anna?' Beth asked.

'As long as you make sure the ponies can't reach anything they shouldn't eat, then yes, I'm sure they would like that.'

They cleared away the empty soup bowls. 'Come on, girls, let's get going. Lots to do.'

With a steadying hand from Grandpa, Niki reached over the banisters to fix the star to the very top of the tree, Beth wound the fairy lights round and round while Lolly concentrated on hanging her favourite baubles lower down.

'Here's Santa in his sledge, and the little mouse with the long tail. I'd better put that one a bit higher so Minou doesn't try and catch it. The wooden rocking horse goes here, and the funny Santa with the long dangly legs needs lots of space,' Lolly talked to herself as she worked.

Beth found the shiny coloured balls to hang, and the bells covered with glitter. They saved the long strands of beads and bells till last.

'Gosh that does look pretty with the lights on,' Granny said as she came in with armfuls of presents, already wrapped. 'Can you put these under the tree for me please.'

All three girls scrambled to see whose names were on the gift tags.

'Oh, there aren't any for us,' Lolly said disappointed.

'Aren't there? Oh, dear, I must have forgotten to get you anything,' Granny said, giving her a big hug.

9

The sisters were having breakfast on Christmas Eve when Anna joined them.

'I've just been talking to Mrs Dunlop, the Pony Club District Commissioner,' she said, grabbing a bowl and helping herself to porridge.

'Gosh, this is a bit thick, I'll need a knife to cut it. Anyway, Mrs D rang to remind me that they're holding a mounted carol service at lunch time for everyone and as you're temporary members, she wondered if you'd like to go. I have to practise my dressage with Summer for our musical display, but Mervyn's grand-children are riding from here and will show you the way. If you'd like to go, Niki must promise not to let

Bracken gallop off, and you'll both have to keep a close eye on Lolly.'

Lolly pouted at the thought of being looked after but cheered up when Beth whispered, 'Don't worry. Niki will be far too busy controlling Bracken to boss you around. You can ride with me instead.'

'What are these children's names?' Niki wanted to know.

'How soon do we have to leave? Have I got time for another slice of toast?' Lolly added.

'Oh yes, plenty of time to finish breakfast. Kerry is the same age as you and her brother Josh is about Beth's age. I'll ring Mervyn and say you'll meet them at the top of the drive at 11 o'clock. You'll need to take some sandwiches and wrap up warmly. It's jolly cold outside.'

'When will it finish 'cos we want to decorate the stables before Mummy and Dad arrive?'

'In that case, I'll borrow Emma's lorry so you won't have to ride home.'

Lolly led the charge upstairs to change into their johds, warmest fleeces and two pairs of socks each. Granny made sandwiches to put in their coat pockets and tucked scarves round their necks.

'Here's some tinsel to wrap round the bridles and thread through their tails.' Anna helped the girls decorate the ponies.

'Have you any antlers for Magic?' Lolly asked.

'No, sorry. I did have some but Bracken ate them years ago and I didn't get more as Summer would have refused to wear them.'

'Must I be on the lead rein? Magic and I were fine yesterday without it.'

'Mmm. I suppose we can tie it round Magic's neck if you promise to let Beth take it if she's naughty.'

'Oh thank you, Anna. I promise,' Lolly gave her a delighted high five.

At last they were ready and Anna rode up the drive with them until they saw Kerry and Josh waiting patiently, then she headed a reluctant Summer towards the manège.

'See you later kiddos. Enjoy the carols,' she called, waving.

Kerry led the way across the forest on her steady pony Shadow, with Niki dancing around on an over-excited Bracken. Josh was rather shy but smiled and chatted as they trotted down the forest tracks, jumping ditches and logs as they went. All the ponies had tinsel in their manes and tails so they looked very festive.

At last Round Hill car park came into view and they joined the crowd of riders, cyclists and walkers who were gathered around the Vicar in his surplice. Song sheets were handed out, and the Vicar announced the first carol. Ponies fidgeted with their bits while their riders sang.

After a few carols, helpers handed round hot drinks and mince pies and the girls ate their sandwiches, sharing them with the ponies.

'You'd never think ponies would like chocolate spread sarnies, would you,' Beth confided in Josh.

'My Toffee will eat anything; I'm sure he thinks every meal is his last,' he answered.

There were prayers and more carols, and just as Lolly was saying, very loudly, 'I can't feel my feet or my nose, or my ears,' Anna arrived driving Emma's horse lorry.

'It's getting colder by the minute, so I thought Kerry and Josh might like a lift home, as a thank you for showing my mob the way here,' she said.

'What a great idea. We're all frozen solid and I expect the ponies are too,' Niki replied.

'Right, we'll leave the saddles on to keep them warm and put their headcollars on over the bridles. Let's get them loaded, then you can go and thank the Vicar and Mrs Dunlop and we'll be off.'

The children quickly warmed up as they rushed around, loading the five ponies, finding Mrs Dunlop and saying goodbye.

'Thank you for a lovely service. See you at the Show next week. Happy Christmas everyone.'

The younger children made themselves comfortable in the living area and Kerry and Niki belted up in the cab. As Anna drove, Niki turned to her, saying, 'Kerry introduced us to Dan and Jeni Young, the agister's children. Dan asked if Kerry and I would like to help him at the Point to Point races on Boxing Day. We'd wear special tabards and be around to make sure the riders go the right way. If Kerry is allowed, can I go too, please?'

'I expect so, if Kerry is going to be there. I'll check with Mervyn and take you both in the trailer if you like,' Anna answered.

'What about us?' Lolly demanded from the 'living' area behind the driver's seat. 'What about Beth and Josh and me?'

'I think you'd better be on foot as the races are very fast and you don't know the forest that well. Also it'll be cold and there's lots of hanging around – worse than today.'

Lolly hadn't wanted to be left behind, but she didn't want to be cold again either.

'Happy Christmas and see you Boxing Day, bye,' they called as Kerry and Josh led their ponies back to Mervyn's stables behind his forge.

The sisters turned the ponies out while Anna returned the lorry, then they raced across the lawn and jostled for the best place by the Aga before sitting down to a late lunch of cottage pie and beans, washed down with hot chocolate.

'Oh what a pretty tree. Now, coats on everyone; we've just time to decorate the stables before bringing in the horses and tucking them up for the night,' Anna said as she came into the kitchen with strings of tinsel and big red and green ribbons tied in bows.

'Do you think you can do something artistic with these Beth?'

'Oh yes, we can hang them around the doors and drape them from the gutters.'

Frost was sparkling on the ground and the horses were waiting impatiently at the gate tossing their heads and stamping their hooves when the girls called out to them. Summer neighed loudly and the others whinnied or whickered.

'Come on,' Anna said as she opened the gate. 'Let's get them into the warm.'

The ponies jostled each other in their hurry to get into their stables where haynets and buckets were all ready for them. Heavy outdoor rugs were changed for warm quilted stable rugs and each horse was given extra pats and carrots.

'They've worked quite hard these last few days,' Anna said. 'I think they deserve their rest tomorrow.'

'Night night ponies. Sleep well. Christmas day tomorrow.'

'Doesn't it look festive with the moonlight shining on the tinsel? Brr, it's cold.'

'Wonder what time Mummy and Daddy will arrive.'

'Quite late I 'spect, it's a long drive and it'll take them ages to pack the car with all our pressies,' Lolly said hopefully.

The Christmas tree lights shone brightly through the windows as they crossed the lawn and went into the welcome warmth of the kitchen. Granny had laid the table for their traditional Christmas Eve supper of scrambled eggs with ham and cheese on thick slices of toast.

'Hurrah, scrambled brains,' Lolly shouted.

'If you have your baths straight after supper you can come back down to wrap up presents while we wait for your parents,' Granny told them.

'Thanks Granny,' the girls shouted in chorus as they thundered upstairs.

10

The kitchen was fragrant with the smell of cooking when they came down in their dressing gowns and slippers, still glowing from their baths. Granny had laid out wrapping paper, ribbons, gift tags and Sellotape.

'I don't want you to see what I'm wrapping,' Niki said, taking paper and ribbons and tucking herself away behind Grandpa's chair.

'Will someone help me please,' Lolly said, struggling with the kitchen scissors. 'No, not you, Beth, you mustn't see. It's a surprise.'

'Here, let me help, I've only got a few left to wrap,' Granny sat beside Lolly. 'Anyone else need assistance? I assume you've done all yours,' she spoke in Grandpa's direction, as he hid behind the newspaper.

'None to do,' he replied.

'I hope you have,' Granny was quite indignant. 'Otherwise you had better lend a hand to Niki and Beth.'

Carols from Kings College choir filled the room as the girls wrapped presents then put them under the tree.

Beth stretched out on the rug, with her arm round Charlie, Lolly sat on Grandpa's lap watching TV while Niki helped Granny to tidy the table.

'I'll leave these out in case Mummy and Daddy need them, then we'll have our hot milk while we wait for them. Gosh, the pile under the tree looks as though we've bought presents for the whole world.'

Niki settled on the window seat so she could watch the drive.

'Finished at last. I wonder if the horses are asleep yet. We hung stockings up outside their stables, but didn't put the carrots in 'cos they would smell them.'

Everyone dozed in the warmth from the Aga. Minou joined Niki on her cushioned seat, Granny and Anna peeled vegetables and stuffed the turkey, Charlie slept under Beth's warm arm while Lolly and Grandpa both nodded off in their shared armchair.

Suddenly Niki leapt up, dropping Minou on the floor

as lights swept up the drive and across the windows. Wheels crunched to a halt on the frosty gravel.

'They're here. They're here,' she yelled, rushing outside and reaching the car almost before Mummy had opened her door.

'Hello lovey. Goodness, I'm sure you've grown in the last week,' Mummy exclaimed giving her a big hug before Niki dashed into her father's arms.

'Humph,' he said lifting her up to kiss her. 'You've surely put on weight.'

By this time Beth and Lolly were also being hugged and kissed.

'Have you brought any presents for us? Have you, have you?' Lolly demanded, dancing up and down.

'Shush, you shouldn't ask for presents, you should just be glad to see Mummy and Daddy,' Beth tried to quieten her.

'But it's Christmas so they must,' Lolly peered into the car.

'Indoors everyone, far too cold to stand around out here. Your Dad and I will unload the car if you go in,' Grandpa said sternly, shooing them inside.

'The roads were very busy but we made good time,' Mummy answered Granny. 'A hot drink would be lovely. What a fabulous tree – did you decorate it yourselves? It does look festive,' she admired the tree as the children clustered around her.

'I put the star on the top.'

'And I hung all those shiny balls and bells and the special things.'

'Grandpa helped me with the lights – they're so pretty.'

At last everyone settled down with hot drinks; Niki leaned against her Dad, Beth sat at Mummy's feet while Lolly climbed onto her lap; even Minou stopped looking indignant and lay down next to Charlie in front of the Aga.

Daddy gave a great sigh. 'It's good to be here. We've been looking forward to our holiday all week. Hope you haven't planned too much for us,' he said, tweaking Niki's hair as the girls chattered about the Christmas fair, riding on the forest and the carol service.

'On Boxing Day I'm helping at the Point to Point,' Niki said importantly.

'Then there's the jumping show and Anna's taking us to the Children's Meet,' Beth added.

'She said I have to be on the lead rein but I want to ride on my own,' Lolly muttered.

'If Anna says you stay on the lead rein, then you must. She knows best,' their mother said firmly. 'Now, time to hang up your stockings and go to bed. Come on, the sooner you go to sleep, the sooner morning will come.'

'And no waking us at the crack of dawn,' Dad called after them.

'I'll help you bring everything in now they've gone up,' Grandpa offered.

The adults sat around chatting quietly, waiting for the murmurs and sshhing from upstairs to cease. There were important things for them to do before they could go to bed themselves.

Of course, Lolly was the first to wake and jumped up and down on the big bed she shared with Beth.

'Wake up, wake up. It's Christmas at last. Has Father Christmas been? Has he? I can't find my stocking – oh, no, my stocking's gone,' she cried as she shook Beth awake.

'I 'spect all your jumping around knocked it on the floor. Go to sleep. It's still night,' Beth muttered pulling the duvet over her head.

But it was no good. Lolly was searching noisily all around the bed and had woken up Niki.

'Wasa time?' she croaked. 'Six o'clock. Far too early Lolly. Oh, all right, let's open our stockings then we can snuggle down again before going to feed the horses with Anna at half past seven.'

Their room was still warm from the Aga chimney, and they wrapped their duvets around them as they emptied their stockings. Nuts, an orange and chocolate money as usual. Niki found a new hoof pick, the Pony

Club Manual of Horse Care, a set of pens and a new pencil case.

'Just what I needed; the guinea pigs ate my other one,' she said happily.

'I've got some new ribbons and hair slides, a sticker book and a hoof pick too,' Lolly said.

'That makes one hoof pick each, thank goodness they're different colours,' Beth said. 'I've got some pencils too and a book on different pony breeds. Look, here's Magic under Welsh Section A.'

'Oh, let's look. Try N for New Forest. The picture looks just like Bracken – not the same as Ginger though, she's much lighter.'

'Is there a Summer? Look, it says this is a Russian Trekehner stallion. Summer isn't quite so majestic but she is black.'

The three children cuddled down again, happily eating chocolates and reading their books until Anna popped her head round the door.

'Wait for us, wait for us, won't be a minute,' Niki hopped across the room trying to put on her socks.

'I'm ready,' Lolly jumped up. 'I dressed earlier.'

They struggled into their coats and boots before heading out into the cold morning, Charlie racing ahead of them across the frosty lawn.

'We'll put outdoor rugs on top of the ponies' stable quilts and let them out but leave the field gate open so they can come in to eat their haynets and shelter from the wind when they want to. That way we won't have to worry about them again until this afternoon. Here are some carrots and they can have an extra apple each as a Christmas treat.'

Niki broke the ice on the water trough by bashing the bottom of a bucket on to it, then helped Lolly rug up Magic. Anna opened the gate and Summer rushed through, eager to stretch her legs followed by Bracken who nipped the mares' hocks and snaked his head to make them canter. Snorting and blowing they cantered around the field with Summer cracking her nostrils, before lowering their heads to the crisp grass.

'Come on. Quickly muck out and fill the haynets then we can have our breakfast,'

'See you later, ponies. Happy Christmas. Come on Charlie.'

'Happy Christmas, lovies. It looks cold out. Come and sit down,' Granny said, starting to dish out the creamy porridge.

'We need to wake up Mummy and Daddy first. Don't 'spect we'll be long,' Niki said as she led the charge up the stairs.

'Heavens, they sound like a herd of elephants. Just a tad excited?' Granny murmured.

'Happy Christmas, Mummy. Happy Christmas Dad.

We've fed the ponies, it's time to get up.' Three bodies landed heavily on their parents' bed.

'Ouff. Gerroff,' Dad squirmed under their weight. 'Ok, ok, we're coming. Has Father Christmas been? Did he fill your stockings?' he added, as he carried Lolly down the stairs followed by Niki and Beth holding their mother's hands.

'Oh yes, and he drank his sherry and ate his mince pie, and the reindeer must have eaten their carrots too.'

'Here's the plan,' Granny said while they were all still at the breakfast table. 'The turkey is already in and the vegetables are prepped, so we can all go to the 10 o'clock church service. Then we can open our presents.'

'Hurrah, goody, yes please,' the children shouted in chorus.

'Lunch after the presents, then we can pop next door to give Mrs Ambridge and Mrs Mavis theirs before tea.'

'Can we go and see Mervyn too? We've got presents for him and for Kerry and Josh.'

'Yes of course,' Granny replied, stacking the crockery in the dish washer. 'Right, best bib and tuckers everyone; we'll need to leave for church by half past nine to be sure of finding seats.'

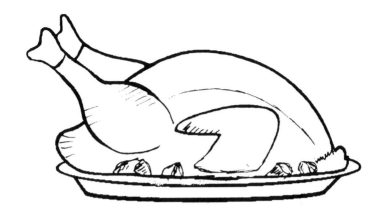

11

'Oh I do love Christmas,' Beth said as she snuggled into her mother's side in the church pew. 'Everyone looks so happy, and the church is lovely with all the holly and berry decorations.'

The congregation sang the traditional carols lustily and luckily the sermon wasn't too long.

'I expect the vicar wants to open his presents too,' Lolly said to the amusement of those around her.

'Can we say hello to the ponies on our way home. I've got a carrot in my pocket for Ginger,' Beth said, taking Anna's hand.

'We'll all go and say hello,' Dad replied. 'Mummy and I haven't seen your new pony yet.'

Bracken was in the yard and Summer was dozing in the open doorway of her stable, but Ginger and Magic were nowhere to be seen.

'Where are they?' Beth cried. 'Where can they be?'

'Sshh, come quietly,' Anna beckoned her to the open stable doors. There were Magic and Ginger, lying down fast asleep in their stables, happy that Bracken was standing guard.

'Oh, don't they look sweet,' Beth tiptoed over to Ginger who half opened one eye and lazily twitched an ear. 'You'd better stay outside, we don't want to frighten her,' she said bossily to her parents.

'Hmm, she's quite chestnut, isn't she. Is she very lively?' Dad said.

'Oh, no, she's really gentle and good,' Beth replied indignantly.

'Why should being chestnut make her lively Dad?' Niki asked.

'Well, tradition has it that chestnuts are hot headed and chestnut mares even more so. It's also said that you tell a gelding, ask a mare and negotiate with a stallion.'

'What does 'notiate mean?' Lolly asked.

'Ne-go-ti-ate, Lolly. It means you have to give and take in order to get a result,' Mummy replied.

'Well, in this yard, you have to ask Bracken, who's

a gelding, but both Magic and Ginger who are mares, do as they're told.'

'And Summer must think she's a stallion because she just does what she wants,' Anna said laughing. 'Ginger has settled in very quickly and is good for Beth's confidence.'

'And I don't mind Beth holding my lead rein 'cos Magic doesn't have to jog to keep up like she does with Summer,' Lolly added. 'Now can we please go and open our presents.'

'There's another old saying about white socks,' Anna said as they waved the ponies goodbye and trooped back to the house.

'Oh, tell us please,' Beth said.

> 'One white sock, buy him;
> Two white socks, try him.
> Three white socks, save for another day,
> Four white socks, send him far away.'

'What does it mean?'

'If a horse has a white sock it usually has a white hoof which tend to be weaker than dark ones. So, a horse with white legs or socks, meant weak hooves. Of course, nowadays with better shoeing and special oils you can strengthen the hooves and keep them healthy.

But in the old days a white hoof would split and then the horse couldn't do its job,' Anna explained.

'But Magic is white all over. Does that mean she isn't strong?' Lolly was worried about her darling pony.

'Oh no, she's good and strong all over,' Anna said hugging her.

Mouth watering smells greeted them as they opened the kitchen door. Granny was basting the turkey and checking on the roast potatoes and pigs in blankets.

'Lunch will be ready soon so we've just time to open our presents,' she said.

'Will you hand out the parcels please Niki,' Grandpa said as everyone found a comfortable spot around the tree. Beth and Lolly sat on the rug with Charlie dog between them; Grandpa chose his favourite chair, Dad sat on the arm of Mummy's chair, and Anna and Granny pulled up chairs from the big pine table.

Niki picked up the parcels and read the labels, 'This one's for Anna, and here's one for Mummy, and Daddy, and Beth – here's one for you Lolly...'

Before long the floor was awash with brightly coloured wrapping paper and ribbons which Minou took great delight in pouncing on. Everyone exclaimed with delight, hugging and thanking each other for their gifts. As well as the usual standbys of new socks, a pretty top for 'best', chocolate oranges, books and the presents bought at the Christmas fair, there were the 'big' presents.

'Look what I've got,' Lolly held up her jigsaw with the picture of two heavy horses ploughing. 'Some proper riding gloves and a tablet with games from Mummy and Dad. And a fleece with a white pony on the front, which looks just like Magic. Thank you everyone.'

'I've got some saddle soap and that lovely pink embroidered horse from the Christmas fair. And a cuddly fleece with a ginger horse head on it,' Beth was thrilled.

The grown ups were pleased with their gifts, too, but quieter with their thanks. Grandpa immediately stood up and placed his carved owl in a niche in the wall, opposite his chair, and Granny and Mummy helped each other do up their necklaces. The others had mostly finished opening their presents before Niki was able to start on hers, and she ripped the wrappings off impatiently.

'Yeeya,' she shrieked. 'Look at these books about children riding their ponies, and this pretty necklace with a horse head – thank you Mummy, it's lovely. My fleece has a brown horse just like Bracken – look Beth, it's leaping – and a tablet to play on. Wow.'

'I've got a tablet too, and thank you so much for

the pretty horse – she's lovely,' Beth replied, giving her sister a big hug.

Granny inspected the turkey.

'Lunch is ready; you've just time to wash your hands while I make the gravy then we can all sit down.'

The table looked very jolly with crackers, candles and Granny's best blue and white china.

There was a bottle of champagne (well, sparkling white wine really, Daddy confided) in a cool bucket, and sprigs of holly decorated the snowy white table-cloth. Grandpa sharpened his carving knife as he stood at the head of the table and everyone said, 'Ohh' and 'ahh' as Dad carried over the turkey on its large silver tray.

Bright eyes, including those of Minou and Charlie, gazed at the feast before them; the potatoes were roasted to a crisp golden brown, the pigs in blankets, ('my favourites,' said Lolly), 3 types of stuffings, cranberry sauce, sprouts, mashed carrots and parsnips and two sauceboats of rich gravy.

Anna and Mummy helped everyone to vegetables as plates were passed and they all chatted loudly, determined not to miss out on anything. Crackers were pulled, paper hats slipped over noses, silly riddles and jokes read out, and before long the plates were empty again.

'Now for pudding. We have pink trifle and good old

Christmas pudding. Who would like what?' Granny asked.

'Me for pink trifle please,' Lolly's hand shot up.

'And me.'

'Me too.'

'I think I'll start with Christmas pud, thank you, and then perhaps some trifle,' Daddy said, rubbing his tummy.

Eventually the table was cleared, the dish washer filled, Charlie and Minou given bowls of scraps and the grown ups settled down with cups of coffee while the girls tidied their presents into piles, admiring each other's new treasures.

'Hey, look at the time. We must go visiting. Quick, where are our presents for the neighbours? If we don't go now it'll be dark before we feed the ponies,' Niki said, jumping up.

First they visited Mrs Ambridge and Mrs Mavis, giving them the tea cosies they had found at the Christmas Fair, and thanking them for the chocolates and woolly gloves in return. Then they rushed to Mervyn's house. The girls were delighted when the front door was opened by Kerry and Josh, who were visiting their grandfather's house for tea.

'We've made you something,' Beth said shyly to Josh. 'They aren't much – we ran out of pocket money, but I hope you like them.'

'Oh, friendship bracelets. Thanks a ton. I'll take the brown and green one, and Kerry can have the pink and blue one.'

'They're lovely. Thank you,' Kerry said, putting hers on straight away.

'Where's Mervyn?' Lolly asked. 'We've brought him a present too.'

'He's asleep in front of the fire,' Josh said giggling. 'Shh, we won't wake him if we leave it on his lap.'

'You are coming to help at the Point to Point tomorrow, Niki, aren't you? Grandfer said he'll take Bracken and my pony Shadow in our trailer as we have to go early.'

'Would you like to come with us, Josh? Anna's taking us to the finish so we won't have to leave until about half ten.' Beth offered.

'Oh, yes, please do come with us,' Lolly said, bouncing up and down, making Mervyn wake up with a snort. 'It'll be more fun to have a friend with us.'

'I'll collect you and Bracken about half past nine,' Mervyn warned Niki. 'He'll need a rug to keep him warm before you set off, and you'll need your thickest woolly vest too,' he added laughing as Niki pulled a face.

'Thanks for the cake, we must be going. Happy Christmas,' the girls called as they headed back across the drive to bring their ponies in for the night.

'It's been a lovely day,' Niki sighed that evening, leaning back against her mother's legs. 'I couldn't eat another thing.'

'Me neither. I'm stuffed,' Beth said, patting her tummy.

'I might manage just a little more trifle,' Lolly said.

'You'll be lucky – Dad finished that while he was helping to wash up.'

12

'What are you looking for?' Niki asked Anna next morning.

Anna had scattered old rugs and boots on the floor of the tack room as she delved into the depths of an old metal trunk.

'Ah, here it is,' Anna held up a dark green woolly rug. 'This is the fleece rug Bracken used to wear at shows. If you put it on him over the saddle, and tuck it round your legs, it'll keep you both warm while you wait. I expect you'll be sent off fairly early, to cover the children's shorter races, but there'll still be lots of hanging around.'

'Now the horses are out we'll go and have our

breakfast; then I'll muck out Bracken's stable while you get him ready, Niki. Mervyn won't want to be kept waiting. Tack him up here and put his head collar on over the bridle for travelling. He can wear his boots in the trailer instead of travelling wraps so you've less to worry about at the other end. It'll be very noisy and busy with organisers and probably about 70 horses and ponies entered in the various races.'

'It sounds terrifying. I wish you were coming with me,' Niki said.

'Mervyn will keep an eye on you both, but don't leave Bracken tied up to the trailer on his own, you'll need to make sure someone stays with him.'

Granny put a couple of Mars bars and some sandwiches in Niki's coat pocket and insisted she wore a scarf around her neck.

'Can I take a carrot for Bracken?'

'Better take a couple so you can give one to Shadow too.'

Niki and Bracken were ready and waiting at the gate when Mervyn came up the drive towing the trailer, tooting his horn, with Kerry and Josh sitting beside him.

'All set? In you go,' he said lowering the ramp. 'That's a nice rug,' as Bracken, with his saddle under the rug, whickered to Shadow who was already in the trailer. Josh jumped down quickly.

'Bye. See you later,' Josh, Beth and Lolly waved as the trailer disappeared down the drive.

'It's good Bracken's already tacked up. So's Shadow. I don't like putting on his bridle out in the open in case he gets loose, and Grandfer says there'll be lots of horses milling around,' Kerry said, showing Niki she was wearing her friendship bracelet.

'Yeah, that would be a total nightmare,' Niki replied. 'I've got carrots and a couple of Mars bars too. Have you helped before? Anna says there'll be masses of people.'

'I haven't helped before but Grandfer used to ride in the Veterans Race so I've watched. We go to a car park – you're only told which one on Christmas day – and all the racers have their ponies checked by the vet before the start. They're given numbered tabards and each race has a different colour. The children's and the veterans races are only over one and a half miles so they start first.

The mounted stewards – that's us – take them to the secret starting point which is the right distance from the finish. I don't know exactly what happens after that as I've only been to the parking area and then the finish.'

'The rest of the races are three miles long over the open forest,' Mervyn told them. 'Because you don't know where you're starting from until you get there, the riders have to know their way around the forest pretty well so they can find a route to the finish. You're galloping all the time, across bogs, over streams, across open moors, through woods and enclosures. It's cold and muddy and you have to be careful where your horse puts his feet. At this time of year the tracks are slippery and holes are hidden under puddles. It's surprising how far 3 miles feels when you're racing over rough ground.'

'It sounds very scary. I don't know that I'd like to do it.'

'Ahh, well, your aunty did it a few years back on Bracken. It was an 'orrid wet day and everyone was soaked to the skin before they even started. Young Anna said they were both shivering with cold while they waited for their race to begin, then one of the other riders barged into her and knocked Bracken clean off his feet.'

'Oh, no, what happened then?' the girls gasped, horrified.

'They got up and carried on. They came third – they were still catching up and overtaking the others when they crossed the finish line,' he told them.

'Oh wow. I must ask her about it,' Niki said.

'Wasn't she brave,' Kerry exclaimed. 'I'd be terrified.'

Mervyn drove into a car park crowded with lorries and trailers with horses and ponies tied to them, more horses being led around, people everywhere and barking dogs adding to the chaos.

'We'll leave the ponies in the trailer 'till we find out where and when they want you,' Mervyn said. 'You go on over to that big lorry with the tables inside – that's the secretary. She'll tell you who to report to while I find somewhere to park up.'

Kerry and Niki jumped down from the ancient Land Rover and weaved their way through the throng. Several people said hello to Kerry and asked if she was competing.

'No, Niki and I are stewards today,' she said proudly.

The secretary was pleased to see them.

'We're short of stewards as a couple have cried off. Too much mulled wine yesterday I expect,' she said, handing them fluorescent tabards with STEWARD written across the back. 'How fit are your ponies? Would you be able to help with the adult races?'

'Oh, yes, we'd love to. My Shadow isn't as fast as Niki's Bracken but they are both really fit,' Kerry said.

'My Aunty Anna said I must stay with Kerry. I don't know the forest well enough to be on my own,' Niki added.

'Anna and Bracken, those names ring a bell. Is your aunt Anna Elliott? If she's taught you, I know you'll be up to the job. Go and report to Mr Young; he's that chap over there with Head Agister on his jacket; tell him I sent you.'

'That's cool; I know his son Dan,' Kerry said. 'I wonder if he's racing or helping today.'

Mr Young told them where to meet him in half an hour.

'Mounted and ready to go mind,' he instructed. 'Girths checked and tabards on.'

'He wants us to take our headcollars too,' Kerry told Mervyn.

'Aye, he would, in case you need to lead any ponies. When it's time to go, we'll tie them round your ponies' necks.'

The girls were grateful for the mugs of hot chocolate Mervyn poured from his flask, as it seemed an age before the tannoy came to life with a cough.

'All entrants in Classes 1, 2 and 3 – that's the children and veterans races, gather by the car park entrance. The rest of you rabble need to gather near Reg Young – he's the ugly bloke standing in his stirrups waving his hat at all you ejits who've entered this rotten race today.' Everyone laughed.

'Ok, girls, mount up. Check your girths while I tie your headcollars on. Keep together, and enjoy yourselves,' Mervyn said, patting their ponies's rumps as they rode off.

'Bracken's shaking with excitement, he thinks he's

going racing. I do hope I can hold him,' Niki said nervously.

'Oh look, there's Dan; come on, I'll introduce you,' Kerry said urging Shadow into a trot.

Bracken tossed his head and pranced after her, throwing Niki forwards up his neck as he bunny hopped into canter.

'Hey up,' someone said. 'Here's a fresh one. Thinks he's racing and no mistake.'

Niki tried to smile bravely as Bracken skidded to a halt beside Shadow.

Mr Young counted heads, told everyone they would get their instructions before each race was started, then shouted, 'Everyone here? Let's go.'

The cavalcade set off, some of the riders immediately galloping off while others chose to conserve their mounts' energy, trotting quietly behind the Agister. Dan rode beside Kerry while Niki had to keep turning Bracken in circles to stay with them.

'People kept on asking me where the start is but Dad didn't tell me until just now. We'll probably have to follow after a couple of races have started, to catch any loose horses and mop up if any one falls off. If we're lucky we'll just get to do the course ourselves without any problems, but there are usually a few fallers,' he told them.

When Mr Young finally called a halt Niki couldn't

see anything that looked like a start line, just more forest.

'Right, you stewards wait over by that clump of trees so you're well out of the way. Class 4, line up by me. You know where you're heading? The finish is up by Beaulieu Road; you'll see orange markers before the underpass and then there are ropes to guide you to the finish, but you have to find your own way there. Any questions? Ready, steady GO,' dropping his raised arm as he shouted 'Go'.

A dozen horses sped away across the forest, some following tracks through the heather, others cutting corners and risking rabbit holes in an effort to take the shortest route.

'Gosh, is that it?' Niki, who had watched Anna start at cross country competitions, had expected a proper start line.

'This is one of the oldest Point to Point races in the country. It's over a different part of the forest every time, and my dad thinks about next year's course all year, working out where will be too wet, too hard, too boggy come the following Boxing Day,' Dan explained.

Niki was impressed. 'Your Dad must be really important.'

'Well, he is Chief Agister – that's the person who's in charge of all the people who work in the Forest.'

'Cool! Is he the only person who knows where the race will be?' Niki asked.

'Yeah, no one even knows where the finish will be until the beginning of December, and then they have to phone us on Christmas Day to find out where to park for the start. That way, although you can guess possible routes for a month, no one actually knows which direction the race will come from until the day before.'

'Hey, you lot. I've started 2 races and want you to follow the third lot. There'll be 4 more classes coming after you so keep your eyes peeled behind as well as in front.' Mr Young told them before collecting his next set of riders and wishing them good luck as he set them off.

'OK, off you go, kids.'

Bracken needed no urging as he surged forwards, determined to catch up with the racers. Niki let him gallop to start with, then gradually brought him back to canter, allowing Dan and Kerry to catch up.

'Gosh, he's a handful. Are you sure you can cope?' Dan was concerned when he saw Niki's red face.

'Mervyn told me this morning that he's done this race with my aunt, so I expect he thinks he's racing again. With luck, he should settle down now he's had a gallop,' she replied.

'If he doesn't, we could swap. My chap's pretty sensible,' Dan said.

'You just want a go on Bracken,' Kerry laughed. 'Come on, we're getting left behind, we should be looking out for lost and fallen riders.'

13

'Look, there's someone walking – she must have fallen off,' Kerry said suddenly.

'Right, Kerry you stay with the rider, and Niki and I will look for the pony,' Dan took charge. 'Ask her which way it went.'

The girl said she was fine but the pony had followed the others. Kerry got off Shadow to walk with her while Dan and Niki cantered ahead.

'All the wild ponies will have left the area when the first riders galloped past, so it should be easy to spot.'

'Look, there's a pony wearing a saddle. It looks as though he's caught up in his reins.' They slowed and

Dan dismounted, walking gently up to the horse which let him take hold of his reins without fuss.

'He's cut his leg but at least he can walk. Here comes Kerry; she'll need to walk these two in while we go ahead to follow the others. Don't worry Kerry, the next race and their stewards will come through soon so you won't be alone for long. Bye,' Dan handed the pony back to his rider before cantering off.

Niki didn't like leaving her friend but Kerry seemed quite happy so she swung Bracken round and followed Dan.

'I don't know this part of the forest at all, so please don't leave me behind,' she called as she caught up with him.

Bracken was sure footed over the rough muddy ground, letting Niki relax. Every so often they saw other stewards walking with fallen riders, leading ponies, or just standing pointing the way. Niki heard hollering behind and turning, saw a couple of riders galloping flat out, jumping puddles and bushes, shouting as they came. Niki and Dan waited beside the path for them to pass.

'Go, go, yipee,' they called, racing each other hard.

'They're brothers who hate losing to each other. One or other usually wins. Their sister will be in the Ladies Race I expect. She used to enter the same race as her brothers, but one year she won and neither of them would speak to her for months.' Dan laughed.

Before long they were overtaken by more competitors, one of whom fell off right in front of them when his horse slipped in a muddy patch. Bracken trotted to the horse almost without being asked, allowing Niki to catch it. The rider was very grateful as he checked its legs before swinging back into the saddle and galloping off.

'Are they allowed to carry on if they fall off?'

'Oh yes, as long as the horse is ok and they can catch it,' Dan answered. 'If the horse is hurt we have to get the horse ambulance as close as possible which isn't always easy. But mostly if it's just winded or has a cut it can be walked back or – as with that one – ridden on. Don't worry, he'll stop if he thinks his horse isn't fit to carry on.'

It was a clear sunny day, very cold, and the ground was just right so there weren't many fallers. They caught up with some other stewards who told them a trailer had been sent to collect Kerry's rider and her pony so they turned back to find her.

They were passed by more racing riders before they saw Kerry trotting towards them. Together again, the three children continued towards the finish, waiting in a group with other stewards as the last of the competitors passed.

Niki was amazed to see the massive crowd cheering at the ropes of the finish line.

'Let's canter up to the finish. We might even get a few cheers ourselves,' Dan said and the three cantered in line up the final hill to the finish, through the cheering crowd, to be greeted by Beth, Josh and Lolly who ran alongside them.

'Mervyn's parked the trailer over there. It's been so exciting watching the riders come in – they were all covered in mud and the ponies were sweating and puffing. Some were still racing up the final stretch. But a couple of ponies were so tired their riders got off just before this last hill.'

They all spoke at once, Niki and Kerry recounting their adventures, Lolly insisting on leading a now quiet Bracken, Beth and Josh describing the excitement as the riders came into view at the underpass and wound their way up to the finish.

'Come and meet my sister Jeni, we'll both be at the Children's Meet and the jumping show next week. She'll like having a girl her own age to talk to,' Dan said, waving to a girl who smiled and said 'Hi' shyly to Beth.

'Daddy said he'd treat us all to a hot dog when you arrived. Come on. Let's find him,' Lolly said, always ready for something to eat.

'I need to look after Bracken first, he's worked

hard this morning,' Niki replied, looking for Mervyn's trailer.

Dan and Jeni went to find their dad just as Mervyn came over with Anna.

'We'll look after the ponies if you want to get something to eat. The family is over by the burger van. You can't miss them.'

'I can smell the onions from here. Gosh, I'm starving. Come on Kerry, race you,' Niki said dashing off; the others followed laughing.

Once they were all supplied with burgers or hot dogs, they wandered back to the trailer, chatting all the way. Kerry knew lots of people who stopped to talk to her. Niki was proud to be wearing her Steward tabard still.

'P'rhaps you can help next year, Beth,' she consoled her sister. 'After all, Ginger is much more suited to helping than Bracken. He was very hard to hold at first.'

'Home time. I'm cold even if you lasses aren't,' Mervyn declared. 'The ponies are rugged and loaded so you two hop in. Might be best if you come back with us too, Josh my lad.'

'See you at home,' Niki waved as they trundled past her family who were walking back to the car park.

'Thanks very much for taking me, Mervyn. It was good fun; I learnt a lot and Bracken really enjoyed himself,' Niki said as she unloaded the pony outside the forge.

'See you at the Children's Meet on Saturday. Bye,' Kerry called as Niki led Bracken back to the yard where Anna was waiting.

'We'll check his legs extra carefully then turn him out with the others 'till tea time. He doesn't look half as tired as you. Reg Young, the Head Agister, said you did ok and wondered if you'd like to help again at the Easter races. So, well done,' she praised her niece.

'I would have got lost without Dan. We met his little sister Jeni too, though she wasn't riding. Kerry's nice and so is Josh. I really enjoyed it but now I can hardly feel my toes – or my nose,' Niki said as they headed for the house and the warm kitchen.

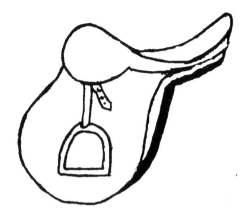

14

'Ow, I'm really stiff,' Niki yawned and stretched before tackling her breakfast. 'Bracken and I need a rest today.'

'It's the Children's Meet tomorrow so Beth and Lolly can just have a quick practise over a few jumps this morning and I shall polish up my dressage to music. If you walk with the girls round to the arena, I'll take Summer later on so Bracken isn't left on his own,' Anna replied.

'Can we come too? We could do with a bracing walk in the cold air,' Dad said.

'Must we? It's freezing out,' Mummy protested,

hugging the Aga, 'I haven't felt my feet since yesterday's Point to Point.'

Beth looked disappointed. 'You haven't seen me ride Ginger yet.'

'Of course I'll come and watch, darling,' she hugged Beth. 'But I would like to thaw my toes first.'

'Greater love hath no mother than to risk frostbite,' Dad laughed. 'How about you, Grandpa? Are you coming too?'

'Ah, no, I think I need to keep an eye on the Aga; don't want it to go out you know.'

'Silly Grandpa,' Lolly exclaimed. 'It can't go out, it's on all the time.'

'Magic is all mine now,' she added proudly. 'I'm off the lead rein mostly now my feet reach below the saddle.'

'Come and watch Ginger, she's so good. She never pulls or goes too fast.' Beth slipped her hand into her mother's as they crossed the lawn to the stable. 'And she lets me catch her every time.'

'Not like Bracken who can be very naughty. Ginger's a bit of a plod really but Beth loves her,' Niki said chattily to her dad.

The ponies had been turned out into the field for the morning and Summer and Bracken made it clear that they did not intend to be caught. However the two smaller ponies were happy to be tempted by carrots. No sooner had they been brought into the yard than the other two bustled over to claim their share of treats. Niki fed a carrot to Bracken and then one to Summer who pushed Bracken out of the way, determined not to be left out.

Mummy watched Beth groom Ginger and Dad helped Lolly tack up Magic. Summer and Bracken whickered softly to their friends as they left the yard.

'Trot around the arena to warm up the ponies while we put up a few jumps for you. Who wants to go first?'

'Me, me,' shouted Lolly.

'I don't mind waiting. Ginger is good at standing still.'

'Slow down Lolly, you're showing off instead of looking where you're... Ooops! Oh dear, I could see that coming.'

Lolly had kicked Magic into a fast canter and not given the pony enough time before the jump so Magic had stopped and Lolly fell off right over the jump.

'I's not crying. Was my fault. Not cross with Magic,' Lolly hiccuped, hugging the pony's neck. 'Sorry Magic.'

'I'll give you a leg up and then we'll start again. Just trot this time until you're both settled, then gently into canter. That's better, go around the arena and then pop over the cross pole first. Remember to lean forward. Good, now turn to the right and over the next jump. Much better. Back to trot, catch your breath,

109

then into canter again and take both jumps again. Sit up, wait for them to come to you, now lean forward over the jump, and sit up again after. That's good. Now go and stand near Daddy while Beth has her turn.'

'It's not fair. You're not telling Beth what to do,' Lolly said, pouting.

'She probably listened to what I was telling you. It sometimes helps to go second; you can watch what to do.'

Anna changed the shape and order of the jumps, raising them when the girls got it right, until at last she said, 'I think that's enough for today. We don't want to tire out the ponies as you'll have a busy day tomorrow,' Anna said as they walked home. 'We'll take the tack into the house so we can clean it in comfort this afternoon.'

It was warm and cosy in the kitchen; the girls and Anna cleaned tack, Grandpa snoozed with Minou on his lap, Granny and Mummy chatted quietly about growing children, school uniforms, cakes and so on, and Dad adjusted the volume of the music recording, startling everyone when he played it back really loudly.

While Beth found Charlie's brush and carefully groomed his long silky coat, Lolly lay on the rug with her sticker book and Niki got out the games board and persuaded Mummy and Dad to play with her. Granny boiled the kettle and buttered scones.

'Have a quick tea before you venture out to bring in the horses,' she said. 'Then get your best riding clothes ready for an early start tomorrow as you'll need to look smart at the Meet. Everyone and his wife will be there.'

'Who's everyone and where does his wife live?' Lolly asked, making the others laugh.

15

It was still dark when Anna woke the sisters.

'We need to feed the horses early today and plait their manes before breakfast. Your Mummy has promised to help.'

They struggled into coats, woolly hats, gloves and wellies before heading to the stables.

'My nose hasn't warmed up since Boxing Day – feel how cold it is,' Mummy bent towards Beth.

'No way. I'd have to take off my gloves.'

The ponies didn't mind having their buckets early and stood quietly eating their hay while they were groomed and plaited. Anna stood on a stool to plait Summer's forelock but the naughty horse kept nudging her with her nose, knocking her off the stool, making it quite clear she would much rather be left alone.

'Gosh, you've done Magic's plaits really quickly. Can you help with Ginger's too?' Beth said admiringly to her mother.

'I get plenty of practise with you three,' Mummy answered. 'Just let me finish here then I'll help you and Niki if she'd like, while Lolly carries on grooming.'

'Do we let them out for an hour?' Niki asked.

'We'd never catch them again. No, they can stay in with their hay – after all, they'll be getting enough exercise later.'

'You'll need to change into your best riding gear – better wear a vest under your shirts – and of course hats and gloves. We'll tack them up here, same as for the Point to Point. Your Dad will follow in the Land Rover, hopefully he won't get lost' Anna said, grinning.

Dad made a face at his sister.

Anna threw on her waterproof coat over her smart riding jacket while the others were still finishing their breakfasts.

'We need to leave by half past nine so get your skates on kiddos. I'm borrowing Emma's lorry so we can take all four horses. I'll go and collect it now and see you shortly at the stables.'

Granny and Mummy helped plait the sisters' long hair.

'No ribbons today – they might be pulled off under low branches,' Granny said.

Dad made sure their boots were polished and helped Lolly put hers on the correct feet. Grandpa stayed out of the way, close to the Aga.

'Can Charlie come with us?' Lolly asked, seeing the big collie sitting by the door looking eagerly at her.

'He can come with us in the Land Rover. You won't want him in the lorry,' Granny answered. 'He'll enjoy meeting all the other dogs and hounds there.'

Niki led the rush back to the stables, where Anna was waiting with the lorry.

'Saddle up quickly and put their headcollars on over the bridles to save time at the Meet,' Anna said. 'Load Bracken first, then Summer so her weight is over the rear axle, then the two smaller ones at the back. Seat belts on and off we go.'

Dad followed with Mummy, Granny and Charlie. The Children's Meet of the New Forest Foxhounds was only a short distance away and Anna used the drive to tell her young nieces what to expect.

'There'll be about 50 children and ponies, some adults "in charge" like me, and the huntsmen in their red coats. Basically, don't get in their way EVER otherwise you'll hear some words which Mummy won't want you to learn. Watch out for the hounds

115

too – Bracken doesn't like dogs around his legs so Niki, you'll need to be very careful he doesn't kick one.'

'What about Ginger?' Beth asked.

'From her behaviour so far I doubt you'll have a problem and Magic certainly won't kick, but you still need to be aware of what's happening around you. I've never taken Summer hunting so we should expect fireworks from her.' The children laughed. 'So I might not be able to look after you all the time. I used to hunt Bracken regularly when he was younger and he can get very excited so I think Beth and Lolly need to stick together like glue as Niki will be too busy to worry about anyone else.'

'Remember, if your pony messes around too much, just get off. Even Bracken will calm down once you've dismounted.'

They arrived at the large lawned area in front of a smart hotel. Anna parked away from the other lorries, leaving space for Dad to pull up alongside.

'Put on your hats and gloves before we unload the horses, so you're ready to mount straight away, in case they start jigging about,' Anna instructed as Dad helped her lower the ramp.

'Crikey, even Ginger looks excited,' Beth exclaimed, as the ponies looked over the partitions, eyes wide and ears pricked at the busy scene in front of them.

Granny and Mummy helped Lolly and Beth lead their

ponies down the ramp and held their heads as rugs and headcollars were removed and girths tightened.

'I'll give you a leg up now before Summer comes careering down the ramp,' Granny said.

Sure enough, Summer nearly trampled Anna, who was very glad that her brother was standing at the bottom of the ramp to steady her and give her a quick leg up. Granny then went back into the lorry to help Niki bring Bracken out.

'At least the ponies are behaving, thank goodness,' Granny said as they watched Summer cavorting around trying to see everything at once. 'Let's walk over to the rest of the riders; she'll be calmer when she's got her friends around her.'

They set off across the lorry park to the green where the huntsmen sat on their clipped hunters; hounds were milling around looking for things to eat and everyone was talking nineteen to the dozen. There were riders and ponies and horses of all shapes, sizes and colours, all looking very smart. Mummy held Lolly's lead rein, Beth rode the other side of her, while Granny, with Charlie on his lead, walked beside Bracken. Dad was by Summer's head, talking calmly to her as she walked tensely, stiff legged, head held high.

'She feels about 18 hands high instead of 16.2,' Anna commented.

'She looks it too from down here,' was Dad's reply.

They halted at the edge of the 'field' to take in the colourful sights and sounds. The 'whippers-in' cracked their long whips in the air to call hounds to them.

'They don't whip the hounds – at least, not unless one is being really naughty when it might be given a tap. Just the sound is enough to keep them under control,' Granny said.

'Hey, Niki, hi, have you just arrived?' Kerry trotted over followed by Josh. 'Isn't this fun? Heavens, Bracken looks even more lively than at the Point to Point. Tell you what, Dan's here too. His pony is fast and he's been before so you could ride with him. His sister Jeni is staying with Josh and me 'cos Shadow is steady. Beth and Lolly can ride with us too if they like.'

'Thanks Kerry, that's kind of you. I was hoping to find someone who could stay in control,' Anna answered breathlessly as her horse tried to turn herself inside out. 'Summer's never hunted before and she's being a bit of a handful.'

'Hello Anna, hello everyone,' Dan and Jeni joined them. 'There's loads more people than last year and the weather's just right for a good scent. We should have a fast run today. You stick with me, Niki, we'll have some fun.'

The hunting horn sounded long and mournful, the Master stood in his stirrups. 'Forward, forward,' he called with a wave of his arm.

16

The field of riders followed him, jostling and chatting excitedly. The larger children pushed to the front with the smaller ones following. Towards the back were very young children on the smallest ponies, being led by their mums or dads. To start with, Summer preferred to stay with her stable mates so Anna circled and bounced alongside Niki with the others following. Dad had been holding Lolly's lead rein but Magic stayed close to Ginger so when the field began to trot, he tied it round the pony's neck.

'If she gets too strong, you can ask someone to hold on, but you should be ok if you stay with Beth,' he said.

Lolly's eyes were out on stalks and her face was screwed up with concentration as she kept Magic close to Ginger with Josh and Jeni on her other side. Now that they were moving Bracken was happily trotting alongside Dan and Kerry while Anna just tried to stay out of everyone's way. The foot followers were soon left behind; Dad ran with Charlie for a while but Granny and Mummy turned back to wait by the car.

Once the Master was sure the children and their ponies were warmed up, he slowed and halted, blowing his horn to encourage hounds to search for the scent which had already been laid by a human 'fox'. Soon the scent was picked up and hounds started to 'sing'. The huntsman blew 'Gone Away' on the horn and hounds lopped off with their noses firmly following the scent. The sound of the horn sent a thrill of excitement through riders and horses alike and the whole field took off across the heath in the wake of the red coat of the Master.

'Remember to stay behind the Master at all times,' Anna called out as Summer made a sudden dash forwards.

'Looks like she's in more danger of overtaking him herself,' Dan muttered to Niki as they sped after her. 'Cor, she's a smashing horse, bet she goes like stink.'

'She's a Trakehner, a proper competition horse. Anna says she's got loads of "character" and that's just being polite,' Niki answered. 'It's a good thing Kerry's pony is quiet, Bracken's too excited to let me look after anyone else,' she added as Bracken put his head down and extended his trot.

'Yeah, Kerry's cool, she'll keep an eye on your nippers as well as mine.'

The field slowed down to go through a five bar gate into an enclosure; then Summer settled just behind the Master as they cantered along the narrower tracks. Bracken knew all about hunting and gradually moved up through the field until he was alongside Anna.

'Ha, might have known he wouldn't stay behind for long. Are you ok Niki?' Anna wasn't really surprised to see her niece, although Niki was too breathless to answer.

'She's just a passenger, Bracken's in charge,' Dan, who had followed, answered for her. 'Good thing he knows what he's doing.'

'Keep your eyes on the Master in case he slows down or stops. It sounds as though hounds have lost the scent.'

Sure enough, the headlong charge through the enclosure slowed with the field bunching up behind the leaders. The whippers-in started hollering and calling to the hounds, encouraging them to cast around to find the scent again.

The stop gave Anna a chance to look round for her

other nieces; she was pleased to see they were still on board, with Kerry in charge. The five children were chatting and waved happily when they saw Anna.

'Thank goodness Ginger has good manners; one less to worry about,' Anna said, waving back. She noticed that although Lolly's face was scarlet she was smiling and Magic seemed relaxed, while Beth was obviously having a great time.

'Hey up, we're off again,' Dan said as one hound began to sing. The others joined in and the pack set off in hot pursuit. The Master blew 'Gone Away' on his horn and the whole field followed briskly.

Being a hunt especially for children, the trail was quite short and after about an hour they found themselves coming back across the open heath towards the lawn where the lorries and trailers were parked. With hounds streaming across the space in full tongue, the field appeared to lose control and galloped hell for leather in their wake. Eventually the Master slowed and so did many of the riders, although some had to turn large circles to steady up. All the horses and ponies were puffing and blowing, still on their toes with the excitement of racing in company.

Once Anna – and Niki – had regained some semblance of control, they looked around for the rest of their party. Dan's pony had started bucking in protest at being asked to stop. Beth and Kerry were comfortable on their quiet ponies, while Lolly, Jeni and Josh had kicked their ponies into a fast canter and followed Anna and Bracken just for the fun of it.

'We'd better walk around to cool them off before we go back to the lorries. Say "Thank you and Good Night" to the Master and any huntsmen you see,' Anna instructed them.

'But it's not night,' Lolly objected.

'No, but it's the correct thing to say. Don't ask me why, it just is,' Anna replied.

'Thanks Dan and you Kerry, for your help. Having friends to talk to made it much more fun.'

'Bye everyone. Will we see you at the jumping show?' the girls called as they went their separate ways.

'Yes, see you then. Bye.'

Even Summer had calmed down by the time they reached the lorry, still hot and sweaty.

'That looked quite scary when you were all galloping back over the green,' Mummy said as she helped Lolly take off Magic's saddle.

'Oh, no, it was fun. But I am tired from trying to stop Magic,' Lolly replied.

'Ginger was a star. I was worried I might lose Lolly and Kerry, but Ginger seemed to know to look after Magic,' Beth said.

'Some kids cried when their ponies wouldn't

behave,' Lolly added. 'But I was brave and didn't cry, even when my toes got cold and my legs were wobbly.'

'I tried to stay with Dan,' Niki told her Dad. 'But Bracken had other ideas! He wasn't going to be left out and just pushed his way through to Summer who was showing off with the Master. That last gallop was great fun.'

'The kids were great; so were the ponies. Summer pulled my arms out until Bracken caught up with us, then she relaxed and we were able to enjoy ourselves. I had been worried about the youngsters until Kerry and Dan joined us; they're really good news,' Anna explained. 'Come on you lot, let's load up and head home.'

'I expect you're all ready for a hot drink and some lunch,' Granny said.

'Oh yes, I'm starving,' Lolly cried and everyone laughed.

'No surprise there,' Dad said.

17

'Check their legs for cuts and scrapes,' Anna said as they unloaded the horses. 'Don't forget to pick out their hooves and offer them water before you put their New Zealand rugs on and turn them out. Perhaps your Dad will look after Summer while I take the lorry back.'

Dad groaned.

'Not the dangerous man-eating horse, please no,' he pretended to beg for mercy while his daughters laughed.

'She's not that bad – especially now when she's had a good run. Here, I'll help,' Niki said confidently holding up each of Summer's legs in turn to check for stones.

They leaned on the gate watching the ponies roll over and over before shaking themselves vigorously and then tucking into the hay spread on the ground.

'My nose has gone numb again,' Mummy said.

'My nose and my toes are numb,' Beth exclaimed.

'My bottom's numb from bouncing on Magic's saddle,' Lolly said, rubbing it.

'Come on you lot, stop moaning. Granny's made a huge turkey stew with dumplings. Last one home's a sissy,' Dad shouted, giving himself a head start.

'Not fair, not fair,' the girls cried, running after him.

Over late lunch in the warmth of the kitchen, they gradually thawed out.

'I wish we had an Aga at home,' Beth sighed. 'Sometimes our house is like an igloo.'

'I'm afraid there isn't room, not even for a small one,' Mummy replied. 'So we just have to enjoy this while we can.'

'Who's going to come and watch my dressage to music tomorrow?' Anna asked. 'I've been given a time of 3.15 so I don't need to go 'till after lunch. The ponies can have a day off to recover from today's antics.'

'Oh yes, can I come please, I want to see Summer dance to our music,' Beth exclaimed.

'I need to watch too so I know what to do when I enter dressage on Bracken,' Niki added.

'I don't want to get cold again,' Lolly pouted; she didn't want to be left behind but she hated hanging around too.

'Tell you what, you come with Mummy and me in the car, then we can arrive to watch Anna, and leave as soon as she finishes,' Dad suggested.

'You'll find it useful to visit the Centre, Lolly, because that's where your jumping show will be,' Anna added.

There was no need to rush the next morning so the girls just let the ponies out and had breakfast before mucking out the stables.

Lolly happily cleaned out the grooming kits while Beth enjoyed sweeping and tidying the tack room, making sure everything was hanging up in the right place. Dad brought his tool box and hung some new pegs, mended the window catch and repaired some damaged fencing. Mummy mended some straps and darned holes in rugs and Niki wrote out neat labels to put under the new – and old – pegs.

'There,' she said. 'Now we know which hook to hang each pony's bridle on, and their headcollars. We each have a peg for our hats and jackets too.'

'Wow, it's so neat and smart. It'll be easy to keep tidy when you're not here to help me,' Anna said.

'Lunch time,' decided Lolly whose tummy was rumbling.

Niki and Beth headed off with Anna towing the trailer. They collected Anna's number while she tacked up Summer, and then had a look around while she was warming up in the outdoor manège.

By the time Anna was ready to enter the indoor arena, the others had arrived and made their way to the viewing gallery where Niki and Beth had been watching earlier riders.

'Daddy has given Anna's music to the lady. She's on after the next one,' Lolly whispered loudly.

'Sshh. Quiet,' muttered Niki to her little sister.

The big doors slid open to let out the previous rider and Anna entered. Summer shied and came in sideways.

'Oh, no. She's going to play up,' breathed Niki, clutching Beth's hand.

'It's all right – Anna knows her little tricks, she'll soon put a stop to her nonsense,' Dad said.

Anna rode the whole way around the arena letting Summer sidle and spook in the corners, then she sat deeply into the saddle, encouraging the horse to behave. Instantly Summer brought her head down obediently, responding to her rider's aids.

The judge's bell rang and just as Anna began her entrance down the centre line, Away in the Manger rang out, and Summer matched her walk to the music. Niki watched the other spectators mouthing the words to the familiar carols as Summer danced in time with the beat; even the judge was nodding her head in time to the well loved tunes.

Summer trotted and cantered to the faster beats of Good King Wenceslas and I Saw Three Ships, then slowed again to walk as Silent Night signalled the finale. The simplicity of the single piano and young voices soared across the arena and when Anna halted in front of the judge for the final salute, the spectators started clapping. Summer knew she was the centre of attention and pranced her way out through the opening doors.

The family rushed out to find Anna.

'That was fantastic. Did you see the judge – even she was singing.'

'Gosh, wow, that was us singing, Mummy. Didn't we sound great?'

'It was lovely, lovely, lovely. You must have won. When will you know?'

'Summer was really listening to the beat, wasn't she.'

'Calm down, girls. I must admit Summer felt great, and the music sounded wonderful. I do hope the judge liked watching us,' Anna was beaming as she patted and hugged Summer.

'Extra carrots for you tonight and I won't get cross even if you try to bite me,' she said to the horse.

'Do you want to go home now Lolly, or shall we wait for the results?' Dad asked his youngest.

'Oh, let's go back inside and watch the others, but no one could be as good as Anna.'

Niki helped take off the saddle and bridle, carefully stowing them in the Land Rover. Anna put a smart fleece rug over Summer to keep her warm and gave her a haynet before pulling warm trousers on over her johds and her clean anorak over her black riding jacket. The lady in the next lorry promised to keep an eye on Summer so they made their way inside to look at the scores and watch the rest of the class.

'Only two more to ride now so we shouldn't have long to wait. Have you looked around so you know what to expect tomorrow?'

'Yes and we've even found the toilets,' Niki replied. 'It's quite a small arena for jumping, I hope Bracken won't trip over.'

At last the class finished and all the riders and their supporters gathered around waiting for the results to be displayed.

Lolly had been upset at the One Day Event during the summer holidays, when she thought Anna was last because her scores were low, so this time she checked with Anna before wriggling her way to the front of the crowd.

'High score wins today, high score today,' she repeated to herself, looking for Anna's name in the list of riders.

'Anna Elliott. Summer. 78%. 1st. Anna, you won, you won,' she shouted, jumping up and down in her excitement.

The crowd laughed to see her bouncing up and down, but Anna was embarrassed.

'Sshh. Quiet Lolly. Not fair on the others,' she hugged the small girl. 'But I am pleased. In fact, I'm as chuffed as chuffed can be.'

'Chuffed as a newt. Chuffed as a bird. Chuffed, chuffed, chuffed,' Lolly sang as they headed home.

18

Anna went over the plan for the jumping show when everyone was in the kitchen having breakfast.

'Beth and Lolly are in the first classes but Niki's is after lunch so we'll just take Ginger and Magic in the morning. Then I'll bring them home and collect Bracken for the afternoon. That way Summer won't be left alone and the ponies won't get too cold hanging around.'

'Do we have to plait?' Niki asked.

'No, not for jumping.'

'It's a good thing we cleaned our tack yesterday before your dressage,' said Lolly who would try anything to avoid chores.

'Yes and a good thing Granny washed your johds too,' Mummy said. 'They looked as if you'd got off and rolled in the mud at the hunt.'

'I couldn't help it, the hounds kept jumping up on me and Magic's only small.'

'Beth and Lolly had better come with me in the horse trailer. Will you go with Mummy and Dad in the car, Niki?'

'Um, no, I think I'll come with you so I can help. But Dad can bring me home to catch Bracken so we're ready and waiting for you.'

Beth didn't take long to groom Ginger but Magic was as muddy as Lolly's johds.

'I can't get Magic clean – she looks as if she's never seen a brush,' Lolly said crossly.

Summer and Bracken watched from the field as the trailer trundled down the drive with their friends.

'Oh look, there's Mervyn's trailer with Kerry and Josh in front of us. Can we park next to them?' Beth was pleased to see her friends.

There were plenty of trailers already parked up and the girls were happy to see several faces they recognised from the show last summer holidays as well as the Children's Meet.

'Will you two tack up Magic while Lolly and I walk the course? We won't be long,' Anna asked.

'Now you've seen the course, do you want to be on

the lead rein or on your own?' she asked Lolly who looked thoughtful.

'Umm, can I do two classes, one on the lead and one on my own?'

'Ok, we'll enter you for Lead Rein, then you can do Minimus same as Beth, then her second class can be Under 10's. That leaves Niki to do "12 and Under" and Small Open this afternoon.'

'Anna, Dad says he'll run with Lolly for Lead Rein, so you'd better show him the course too,' Niki and Beth thought this was very funny, and were keen to watch.

'That's great, Magic went so fast last year I couldn't keep up with her. Good luck.' Dad rolled his eyes as Anna patted her brother on his back.

Lolly mounted and took Daddy into the outdoor school to warm up over the two small jumps.

'You must keep hold of the lead rein all the time,' she told her father seriously. 'Otherwise I'll be 'squa-filied.'

When it was Lolly's turn, the rest of the family crowded into the viewing gallery to watch and cheer. Dad nearly forgot to wait for the bell but Lolly shouted, 'Not yet, Daddy, wait for the bell,' so loudly that the spectators chuckled.

Then they were off; over the first one, Lolly yelled 'turn turn' to her father and he and Magic jumped together, before racing for the third; Magic began to inch ahead of Daddy who was puffing as he ran and jumped, with the lead rein getting ever longer.

'Don't let go, hold on, hold on,' Lolly shouted. Daddy sank to his knees as they crossed the finishing line.

'Please tell me there isn't a jump off,' he gasped.

The ring steward grinned. 'No, we wouldn't do that to you. We always time the first round of this class otherwise none of the dads would take it on.'

When the results were read out, Lolly was delighted to have come second, although she did blame Dad for them not winning.

'Sorry, pet, I just couldn't go any faster. I've got a bone in my leg which slowed me down,' he said, tossing her into the air.

'Put me down, Daddy. This is Pony Club,' Lolly said with dignity. 'Anyway, it's time for the next class and I want to watch how Beth does.'

Anna had advised Beth as they walked the course together.

'Ginger likes to go steadily so cut corners to keep your time down. Try to go inside this red and white fence to reach the blue one at an angle and cut back to the left, then three strides and over the wall. You'll need to be straight for the double but then a sharp turn will take you over the last. Remember to look at the next jump before you land so Ginger knows which way to turn.'

'Good luck,' she added sending them forwards with a pat on the pony's rump.

'Must wait for the bell, get into canter, there's the bell, and we're off,' Beth talked to her beloved pony all the way round, as they twisted and turned between the jumps, sometimes seeming to need only a couple of strides before taking off.

'Well done, that was brilliant. She is a good pony,' Anna greeted her as they came out. Beth grinned happily.

'My turn now. Me now,' Lolly pushed forwards.

'Remember, it's the same course just a bit higher, so Magic will know the way but you need to tell her all the same. Don't try and go too fast or you'll miss the jump by that dark corner at the other end.'

Lolly was full of confidence and put Magic into canter. Fortunately the bell went before she crossed the start line as she had forgotten to wait for it. She kicked the pony over the first jump and they flew towards the next. A sharp turn across the arena and over a couple more jumps, by which time Magic was going so fast they missed the turn out of the corner and had to circle back to take the jump.

'Sorry Magic, I forgot what Anna had told me,' Lolly was nearly in tears as they finished the course.

'I was so stupid. Magic just flew and it was such fun that I forgot to slow down.' She was cross with herself.

'At least you've got a rosette from the first class. Anyway, it's your first time off the lead rein,' Mummy comforted her. 'Here, let me help with Magic now you've finished.'

The jumps in the Minimus class were very low and Beth was not placed – some of the riders had gone really fast.

'The Under 10 class is higher, so accuracy will be more important than speed,' Anna coached her before she went into the indoor school for the second time.

Ginger seemed to perk up as she headed for the first jump and Beth felt they were moving more quickly than before. She had to concentrate really hard to keep up with the pony, turning sharply and taking some jumps at an angle, then sitting up for the double, before cantering steadily down the final line of jumps.

'Clear round again. Well done. Lots of riders are getting careless on that last line so they're having one or two down,' Anna greeted her. 'And your time was good too. We'll keep our fingers crossed for a placing this time.'

'I'll take the ponies home while you wait for the results. Niki's already gone with Dad to get Bracken ready,' she added.

19

As Anna parked, Lolly and Beth rushed out to meet them, with Beth waving a yellow rosette.

'I came third, I did, I came third. Wasn't Ginger wonderful? I can't wait to tell her this evening.'

'She's a good little pony, but you had something to do with it too,' Anna laughed.

'That's one rosette each. Now it's your turn Niki,' Lolly said bossily.

'No pressure then.' The adults laughed as Niki made a face at her little sister.

'Go away, I don't need any help and I don't want you hanging around,' she said crossly.

Mummy and Dad took the two younger girls into

the viewing gallery with strict instructions not to say a word, especially when Niki came in. Anna walked the course with Niki and then watched as she warmed up Bracken in the outdoor school.

It seemed an age before it was Niki's turn by which time she couldn't feel her fingers or toes they were so cold. The steward called out her name and she headed to the arena in a daze.

Anna could see that Niki was nervous.

'Niki. Stop. Look at me. Deep breath,' Anna halted her, bringing her back into focus. 'That's better. Off you go and remember to enjoy it.'

Niki gulped, gathered the reins, then breathing deeply gave Bracken a gentle kick.

'Come on boy, let's do this.'

She cantered into the centre of the arena and turned towards the first jump when she heard the bell. Bracken leapt over the first with an almighty bound, almost unseating her, but Niki managed to stay on and then they were safely over the second. She remembered to look towards the next jump before they landed, and Bracken turned sharply, taking only two strides before it. She steadied him out of the corner sitting up straight for the double.

The last line of jumps down the side of the arena were just too inviting and Bracken picked up so much speed he knocked the last pole. The spectators held their breaths as the pole wobbled and bounced in the cups before at last falling with a loud thump.

Niki was upset. 'It was my fault. Bracken was great but I didn't keep him steady down that line and we dropped the last.'

'You got lucky because you'd crossed the finish line before it fell, so it counts as a clear round. Just think of it as a wake-up call,' Anna was stern.

Niki was warming up for her second class when the tannoy crackled into life, announcing the results in reverse order. She heard her name but didn't know where she had come.

'Niki, Niki, you've come third in the 12 and Under class. Aren't you pleased? Go and collect your rosette – it's yellow like mine,' Beth shouted at her.

'It'll have to wait, I'm busy now,' she replied.

Before she entered the arena Anna spoke quietly to her.

'This is the "Small Open" class which means any rider up to the age of 14, on any size horse. You've jumped this height many times before but you'll be up against some good ponies. Just remember to head Bracken towards the jumps and he'll do the rest. Treat it as a schooling round and enjoy yourself. Don't ride against the clock, concentrate on trying for a clear round.'

Niki nodded, took a deep breath and rode into the brightly lit arena.

She cantered and circled until the bell went, then aimed for the first jump. The first class had taken the tickle out of Bracken's toes so he was happy to glide smoothly over the poles. Niki sat back up looking towards the second jump. Bracken adjusted his stride and flew over it. They had to change direction for the next few jumps and Niki brought him back to trot so he could rebalance himself in readiness for the double. A quick pull on the reins saw him shorten his stride for the corner, then the narrow stile set at a sharp angle.

'Come on, Bracken,' she whispered,' Just these three to go. Carefully does it.' Remembering their previous round, Niki sat up, making the pony wait for each jump to come to him and they cleared the last.

'Well done, well done. Not fast but beautifully ridden. I'm proud of you,' Anna said as they trotted out of the arena.

The girls helped put away Bracken's saddle and load him into the trailer while Dad and Mummy went with Niki to collect her rosette from Mrs Dunlop, the Pony Club District Commissioner.

'Hello, you again. I've already given both your sisters rosettes today. I can see it's going to be just like when Anna was in Pony Club; she rarely went home empty handed. I'm so glad you joined us this week. I hope you'll become full members this year, then I can send you the schedules in advance.'

'That would be great, can we join Mummy, please?' Niki asked.

'We have a special rate for families – if you can wait a mo I'll find the forms...' Mrs Dunlop searched through a pile of papers to find the appropriate piece of paper.

'Here we are. No need to fill it out now. Just return it to the address at the bottom – with your cheque of course. Or scan it and send it on line to our web site with your card details. Ha, ha. Most important. Mustn't forget that,' she thrust the form at Mummy and with a final 'Jolly good,' dashed off to catch another un-suspecting parent.

'It doesn't seem very expensive and now the girls are here every holiday they'll make more friends too,' Mummy said, quickly reading the form.

The sisters were delighted and gave their parents big hugs before jumping into the cars and heading home.

They were tucking into their favourite supper of 'spaghetti worms' when the phone rang. Granny came back with a big smile on her face.

'That was Mrs Dunlop. You left before the final class places were announced. You came 7th Niki and she says she'll put your lilac rosette in the post.'

'It's been the best Christmas ever,' Beth said as they snuggled down into their beds that night. 'First we had snow, then Anna gave me Ginger.'

'And Magic is all mine now with no lead rein, except sometimes,' Lolly added.

'Then,' Beth went on, 'we sang for Anna's music, and we rode lots.'

'Saw Santa at the Christmas fair and had presents and fetched the tree,' Lolly interrupted again.

'Took the ponies to the carol service, and put up the Christmas decorations and Mummy and Dad arrived and we had lots and lots of presents,' Niki butted in.

'And pigs in blankets and turkey and pink trifle,' Lolly murmured quietly as her eyes closed and she slept.

'All the excitement of the Point to Point – I'd love to help at the next one,' Beth took over again.

'The Children's Hunt was great, I really enjoyed that. Bracken's a bit strong but Dan thinks he's cool.'

'Ginger is super cool, too. I wasn't nervous at all and I like Kerry, she's really nice.'

'Then today we all won rosettes and can join in the Pony Club rides and stuff next hols.'

'Mmm,' Beth was sleepy now. 'Ride tomorrow on the forest then home and back to boring school.'

'We'll have lots to tell our friends. Roll on Easter.'

They both fell asleep.

20

The Christmas holiday ended with so much ice is wasn't safe to ride. Back home in the midlands town of Ashton, the winter term dragged, with rain, wind and more rain. Tempers were short, and Mummy struggled to keep up with the laundry and dry out wet shoes and coats.

'Perhaps we could visit Granny for half term?' Beth suggested after yet another argument between the three sisters ended in tears. 'The ponies really need to be ridden. Anyway, I'm missing Ginger dreadfully.'

Mummy sighed.

'I'll ring her this evening, find out if it's possible.' The thought of having a week without the children was quite inviting.

'I'm so sorry, we'd love to have them but I've hurt my arm so can't drive at the moment and Grandpa is down with a nasty cold. It hasn't stopped raining since Christmas and the gateways are knee deep in mud. The field looks like a lake – the heron and egrets from the river have come up to fish for worms. Even the manège is too wet to ride in and the forest so slippery Anna hasn't ridden Summer for a couple of weeks. The ponies are just turned out in the field, rugged up against the weather and Anna is working extra hours so she can take more days off when the girls visit in the Easter holidays.'

'Oh well, never mind. Beth was so looking forward to seeing Ginger again, but she'll just have to wait 'till Easter,' Mummy was disappointed and hated having to tell the girls, but strangely Niki didn't seem to mind.

'I didn't want to go anyway,' she muttered and slunk off to hide in her bed.

'What's up with Niki? She's very stroppy these days,' Beth asked.

'I don't know dear, perhaps it's the weather, I know it's getting me down,' Mummy replied.

The girls took a course of swimming lessons which kept them busy during half term, and Niki cheered up a bit as the life saving was good fun; it included swimming in clothes and rescuing her little sisters who enjoyed pretending to drown.

The rest of the spring term seemed just as wet and miserable. Niki became more silent and stopped visiting friends for tea and snapped at mummy or sulked in her bed. Everyone was fed up; even the thought of chocolate Easter eggs couldn't cheer them up. Beth and Lolly started counting off the days until the end of term when Granny would collect them.

'Only one more week before Granny comes.'

'This is our last weekend before the holidays, I'm going to start packing. I hope I can still fit into my johds. Where are my boots?' Lolly wailed anxiously.

'We left them at Granny's. Don't you remember, they were wet and anyway, you don't need them here,' Beth said.

'Niki, please collect your things as well so I can make sure everything is clean,' Mummy said as she hurried past with yet another pile of washing.

'Don't want to go,' was Niki's response.

'What's the matter with you? You love going to the forest and seeing Bracken. And you've got lots of friends down there – don't you want to see them again?'

'You don't understand. Leave me alone,' Niki muttered and hid under her duvet.

All week, Beth and Lolly chattered about riding, the ponies and Charlie dog. They tried to talk to Niki, but she wouldn't answer. Even Dad got cross with her and insisted that she pack her bag.

'You can't expect Mummy to do your packing for you just because you're in a strop about something. What is it? Why won't you talk to us?'

But Niki just hung her head and turned away.

When Granny collected them from school on the last day, Lolly and Beth jumped around her excitedly, talking non-stop, but Niki just dragged her bag to the Land Rover before getting in and doing up her belt.

'Don't I even get a "hello"?' Granny asked, leaning over to give her 'big' girl a hug.

'Hello,' Niki said reluctantly allowing the hug.

Beth was so excited about seeing Ginger again she didn't stop talking all the way to the forest. Granny had to ask her to be quiet when the traffic was heavy, but at last they reached the familiar, quiet lanes of the New Forest.

'Oh, look at those tiny calves over there – gosh, they're early aren't they. Will there be any foals yet, Granny?' Beth asked.

'It's too early for foals on the forest; I expect those calves were born on farms then turned out when they were a few weeks old.'

Niki sat up and started to take notice. 'The forest looks very wet still. Will we be able to ride out?' she asked.

'It hasn't rained much for a week now, so the ground is starting to dry up. Did Mrs Dunlop send you the Pony Club schedule for the holidays? Do you know what's been organised?'

'We saw it online and Beth's been reading it for weeks,' Lolly said. 'There's something called Stable Management.'

'There's a Beach Ride too,' Niki piped up to everyone's surprise.

'I didn't think you were interested,' Beth said. 'I never saw you looking at the schedule.'

'Well, I couldn't help it, you kept leaving the computer on,' Niki retorted.

'It sounds as though you'll be kept busy. Fortunately Anna has booked the holidays off work so she'll be around every day. Ah, here we are, home at last.'

The girls jumped out of the car as Charlie dog bounded down the steps to greet them, tail wagging, mouth open in a big smile. Grandpa followed more slowly, 'Charlie's been waiting in the window for the last hour,' he said as he hugged each of his granddaughters in turn.

'Don't stand there in the cold, go on in. I'll bring your bags.'

'Can we see the ponies tonight, please,' Beth begged. 'I can't wait to see my darling Ginger.'

'They're out at the moment and Anna isn't back

from work yet so you'll have to stay at the gate. Put on your wellies and I'll have supper waiting for you.'

The girls rushed to the boot cupboard and struggled to pull on their wellies.

'I think my feet have grown lots,' Lolly said.

'Silly, that's last year's pair. Here, have my old ones,' Beth comforted her.

'Last one there's a dunce,' yelled Niki, striding off into the gloom.

All three climbed over the five-bar gate into the yard, and Niki opened the feed room door for carrots to give to the ponies. Ever-greedy Magic was first to arrive, followed quickly by the others who heard her crunching and pushed and shoved to claim their treats. Summer reached over Ginger's back and nipped Beth until she too had a mouthful of carrot, then went back to grazing when the treats were all gone.

Niki sat on top of the gate, hugging Bracken, while Lolly stood on the middle bar to reach over to Magic. Beth leant over so far that she ended up on Ginger's back. The surprised pony just stood waggling her ears.

'It was an accident,' Beth insisted.

'Yeah, accidentally on purpose no doubt,' Niki replied.

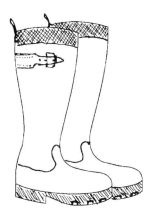

21

'The ponies are still losing their winter coats and haven't seen a brush for ages, so you'll need to give them a thorough groom,' Anna said at breakfast the next day, 'You'll need to check their hooves to see if they need shoeing, then we can pop round to the manège for a warm up session this morning.'

'I'm going to make Ginger the shiniest, cleanest pony in the whole world.' Beth was a tidy sort of girl and the thought of cleaning anything, especially her beloved pony, excited her.

'I'll never get Magic looking white,' Lolly muttered crossly, looking at her muddy pony. She wasn't keen on anything that sounded like hard work.

'I expect Bracken has even managed to get mud inside his ears, but I'll help you when I've done him. Oh look, you can see where Magic's rug begins and ends,' Niki said laughing when the pony's rug was removed. 'Her neck is dirty grey and her body is white.'

'Use the curry comb to take off her winter coat. You'll have to breathe through your noses if you don't want mouthfuls of dust and hairs. Here, Lolly, rub in circles; going against the way the hair grows pulls it out more quickly.'

With the ponies tied up in the yard contentedly munching on hay, the girls set to with stiff dandy brushes and curry combs, removing lumps of mud from the animals' legs and carefully de-knotting their manes and tails. Using their hands they gently rubbed mud off the ponies faces and out of their ears. Dust and hair floated in the air and lay in a carpet on the concrete floor.

'I've a super new comb which trims manes so they look "pulled" but without the pain. Let me show you on Magic. You have to start right at the top of the mane, then run it down the hair in one sweeping motion. The teeth are sharp and thin the mane neatly, giving it that trimmed look without appearing to be cut. Here, you try, but mind your fingers,' Anna gave the comb to Lolly who stood on an upturned bucket to reach the top of Magic's neck.

'Oh, look, a great clump of hair has come off,' Lolly was startled.

'Yes, but Magic didn't mind because it doesn't pull the hair out by the roots. Work down the mane with each stroke, so you get an even look. Well done, she's looking much tidier already.'

'Can I have a go please? Ginger looks as though she's been through a hedge backwards,' Beth was impatient; fortunately Anna had another comb so she didn't have to wait.

'We'll trim tails while they're doing the manes,' Anna said to Niki. 'First put your arm under the tail at the top, so you're holding it in the same position the pony does when it's walking. Then work your other hand down the tail. Then you make a straight cut across the bottom. Bracken's tail has grown very long over the winter, but he needs a good length in the summer to help him whisk flies off, so cut half way between his hock and fetlock.'

'My arms aren't long enough for this,' Niki complained. 'Bracken keeps swishing his tail just as I'm ready to cut it.'

'Keep trying. You'll suddenly get the hang of it,' Anna reassured her, going to make sure Magic and Ginger hadn't been left completely bald.

'I think that's enough now Lolly, as Magic's mane is

thinner than the two Forest ponies. Let Niki have the comb for Bracken.'

'Will you trim her tail? I haven't got it very clean,' Lolly said, hoping most of the mud would be cut off or that Anna would finish it for her.

'Hmm, you haven't brushed her hocks clean either. Tell you what, I'll trim her tail and show you how to rub it to remove the dried mud, and you can clean her legs properly.'

'We look like a bunch of Yetis,' Niki said, giggling as she saw her sisters' sweatshirts and jeans covered in hair. 'Lolly looks like an ancient crone with white hair all over her, and Beth looks like a ginger orangutang.'

'Well, you look like a grizzly bear,' Beth retorted.

'It's not fair. Anna hardly had to brush Summer to get her clean and tidy,' Lolly grumbled.

'That's because she's clipped for the winter to stop her getting hot when I ride her,' Anna said, neatly skipping out of the way as Summer waved a hind leg in the air when she tried to groom a ticklish bit. 'You'd better go and change quickly, otherwise we won't have time to ride,' she added.

'But if we turn them out while we're gone, they'll roll and get all dirty again,' Lolly objected. She didn't want to do any more work.

'They can stay in the yard with haynets, otherwise we won't be able to catch them.'

'Especially Bracken, he hates being caught again. Last summer he didn't want to be caught and ran circles around me. He let me come really close then tossed his head and cantered away. I was very cross with him,' Niki remembered how he had teased her.

'But when I caught Magic he followed her into the yard – and he did say sorry to you,' Beth added, remembering how close to tears her big sister had been.

The girls raced back to the house to change into their johds and riding boots.

'Gosh Lolly, you must be full of Christmas pud still, you're johds won't do up,' Granny commented. 'Anyone else outgrown their kit?'

'Help, yes, we all have,' Beth and Niki were both trying to pull up johds that were too short and too tight, and stuff their feet into riding boots which were a size too small.

'Lolly will have to wear Beth's old johds and boots, Beth can have Niki's and Niki will have to wear her jeans and wellies today. Try wearing two pairs of socks to keep the boots on if they're too big. I'll ring Mrs Dunlop; she keeps all the second hand kit. You'll each want Pony Club ties too.'

Beth's johds were only just too big for Lolly, but Niki's were much too big for Beth who had to hold them up with a belt and roll up the legs. At last they were ready.

'Thank goodness our hats still fit,' Beth said as they returned to the stables.

'Let's wave to Mervyn as we pass the forge,' Niki said as they set off up the drive.

Mervyn waved back. 'If those killer ponies need new shoes you better bring 'em on your way home. My lass Kerry says she hopes to see you at the rally next week,' he called.

'All that grooming this morning has made my arms ache. I do hope Bracken doesn't pull too much today,' Niki said as they entered the manège.

'No chance,' the others laughed as he broke into canter even before the gate was shut.

'Oh, well, let's all have a canter to take the tickle out of their toes,' Anna decided. 'I'll just run through my dressage test for tomorrow's one day event, so if you lot want to head back via the blacksmith I'll catch you up there.'

22

'How far away is the competition? What are your times?' Niki asked at lunch.

'It's just a half hour drive, for a change, so I can walk the cross country course this evening. My test is at a quarter past ten, then show jumping is quarter past eleven. We'll aim to get there for nine o'clock to let Summer have time to relax before our warm up.'

'We'll help clean your tack this afternoon,' Beth offered.

'That would be a great – thanks.'

Lolly didn't enjoy cleaning tack and took Charlie off to play in the garden. She put out the dog agility equipment they had used the summer before, and soon had Charlie jumping over old chairs and wriggling under the tarpaulin again. Charlie was walking up an old plank when, to her horror, he yelped and held up his paw which had blood dripping from it.

'Granny, Granny, come quickly. Charlie's hurt,' she shouted, running for the house. Charlie whined quietly as Granny looked at his paw.

'He seems to have cut it on something. Where was he when it happened?'

'He was climbing up that plank,' Lolly answered, pointing.

'Oh dear, there's a rusty nail sticking out. He must have trodden on it. We'll have to take him to the vet. He'll need a tetanus injection and it may have to be stitched too. You'd better come with me,' Granny told her.

'Oh, poor Charlie. I didn't mean him to get hurt. I don't want to go with you. The vet might hurt him, and it's all my fault,' Lolly said, crying.

'But I need you to keep him calm in the car. Now dry your eyes and run to tell the girls where we're going, then we'll leave straight away,' Granny said briskly.

Niki and Beth ran back with Lolly to find that Granny had put a bandage on Charlie's paw and lifted him into her car.

'I'll just take Lolly; the vet won't like too many

in his surgery. Anna will have to think what to do about tomorrow, as Charlie won't be able to go to the competition. He can't be left on his own so I'll have to stay here with him as Grandpa will be out all day.'

Lolly put her arms around the big dog and held him tightly as they sped off to the vet's surgery.

'You'll have to set him a brave example,' Granny told her as they waited their turn to see the vet. 'Let's hope he won't need stitches.'

'What a beautiful dog,' the lady vet said as he limped into her room, holding up his paw pathetically. 'I'll just have a quick look. Ah, yes, it's bled nicely so most of the dirt will have come out, but we'll put his whole paw in this antiseptic solution to make sure the wound is clean, and I'll wrap it in an elastic bandage. Then he just needs a tetanus shot – if you'll hold him still – there, all done. Give him these antibiotic tablets in his meals twice a day. You'll probably need to change the bandage so here are a couple of spare ones. Come back if you're at all worried. Bye.'

Charlie led the way out to the car, keen to leave the vet behind.

'I'm sorry, Charlie,' Lolly murmured into his hairy neck. 'I didn't check the plank for nails. It's my fault you got hurt. I promise I won't forget another time.'

'Charlie's giving a very good impression of a badly wounded soldier,' Anna said laughing, as the dog raised

159

his injured paw with a hopeful expression on his face as they sat down to supper.

'Have you decided what you're going to do about your competition tomorrow. Can you go on your own?' Granny asked.

'I've talked it over with Niki and Beth, and they'd like to come with me. They know what needs to be done as they helped at that event last summer. If Lolly promises to do as she's told and not wander off, she can come too,' Anna replied.

'Well the girls are very sensible these days, so if you're sure they won't be in your way I suppose that'll be all right. I'll have to keep Charlie quiet here at home, so perhaps Lolly could stay and help me with Charlie,' Granny said.

'No, no, I want to go with Anna. Please. I'm so sorry to have let Charlie get hurt, but I really want to go with Anna. I promise to be very good and even do what Niki says,' Lolly said, which made them all laugh.

'That's settled then. You've all promised to be sensible so I'll be glad of your company.'

23

'Wow, what a lot of lorries. Some of them are huge,' Beth said as they drove into the country park the next day. 'And look at that grand house. It's really posh.'

'Yes, this is a popular venue for professional riders as well as us amateurs. It's one of the first in the season because the ground is so well drained the going is always good. This looks like a handy place to park, close to the action,' Anna stopped in a space between two smart lorries.

'What would you like us to do first?' Niki asked.

'Go to the secretary's tent – we passed it on the way in by the show jumping arena – and collect my number please, while I put studs into Summer's shoes and tack up.'

The three girls ran off, gawping at the trade stands.

'We'd better get the number first, then we'll have a quick look at the shops so we know what to look at later,' Niki decided, taking charge.

Summer was ready and Anna had put on her black jacket by the time they came back with her number, which she tied on straight away.

'I need to mount and warm up for my dressage; will you lock the car and follow?'

The sisters had gone to a One Day Event last summer with Granny and Anna so they knew the routine. The competition started with the dressage test, for which Anna wore her black jacket, velvet hard hat, black boots and white gloves, shirt, stock and johds. Her long hair was neat in a hairnet with a black bow. Summer's mane was plaited, her tail shaped and brushed out, her white socks clean and her hooves shiny with polish.

Once mounted, Anna joined the other riders in the warm up area where she gave the horse time to look around and relax before encouraging her to listen and respond to her rider's aids. Niki found a shady spot near the test arena.

'We'll sit here so we can watch without getting in anyone's way,' she said.

'Oh, look at that chestnut flicking out her toes. Wow, she looks as though she's floating,' Beth commented.

'Hmm,' Niki answered, not impressed. 'Wonder what her jumping's like.'

'Summer looks so beautiful with her mane plaited like that,' Lolly was fiercely loyal.

'Look, Anna's going in now. Oh isn't Summer naughty – she's tossing her head and not looking where she's going.'

'At least she hasn't started yet, perhaps she'll settle quickly.'

The judge's bell rang and Anna quietly turned and entered the arena.

'Nice straight entry,' Niki said, sounding knowledge-able.

They turned in front of the judge and continued their test, trotting, cantering, circling, crossing the arena on the diagonal and finally halting before the judge and saluting. Anna walked the horse out of the arena, patting her neck and giving a big sigh of relief.

'I thought it had gone wrong before we'd even started when we passed that stallion,' Anna said as they walked back to the trailer.

'You settled her really well though,' Beth said, remembering that Granny had told them to always find something positive to say.

'Yes, it went ok in the end. I'm quite pleased really. Now I must change her tack and head over to the show jumping. But first I need a drink of water; I was so nervous my mouth has gone really dry.'

Lolly poured the water, Beth put away the dressage tack and Niki handed out the jumping saddle and boots. Working as a team, they soon had Anna mounted again and headed to the show jumping ring for the next element of the day.

Again, Niki found a safe place for her younger sisters to sit and watch, then stood by the jumps in the warm up area, ready to change them as Anna wanted.

She was careful to stand with the other helpers, out of the way of all the horses practising their jumping. At last Anna's number was called and she entered the main arena, cantering around the ring until the bell rang to allow her to start.

The girls watched with bated breath as Summer cleared one jump after another; gasping as she knocked a pole and then relaxing again when it didn't fall. Anna steadied her as they approached the double, shortening her stride so she reached the second jump correctly. Hooves thudding on the grass, Summer powered away towards the final obstacle which she flew before stretching her neck forwards over the finish line.

The girls jumped up, cheering and clapping.

'Oh, well done. Way to go. Hooray.'

They ran to join Anna as she left the arena. 'Wow, she jumped those beautifully. That was so exciting, you looked really fabulous.'

Anna laughed down at them as Summer jogged sideways, cracking her nostrils and breathing hard.

'I really enjoyed that. Summer usually insists she knows best, but today she didn't put a foot wrong and listened to me for a change. We've been practising this new height during the winter and it's really paid off.'

'Are you going to walk the cross country course now? Would you like us to stay and watch Summer?' Niki asked.

'I walked it yesterday evening so I'll sit and have a drink and snack. You can go and watch the other riders but please be back here in an hour. Don't forget to keep an eye out for horses – listen for the fence judge's whistles which they blow to warn a horse is coming,' Anna's voice followed the girls as they ran off.

'Come on, let's watch a couple of horses start then we can follow them round.'

The cross country course was shaped like a figure 8 so the start and finish were close together but the riders wouldn't bump into each other as they galloped round. Some of the jumps were in a small wood so spectators had to wait anxiously for them to come into view again.

Niki led her sisters to a low mound right in the middle of the course.

'We can watch the start from here and we've got a really good view of loads of jumps so we don't have to walk the whole way round.'

'Oh, look, that one doesn't want to go into the start box. What a fuss it's making,' Beth said.

'You'd think they'd practise before coming to a competition, but perhaps it's young and nervous,' Niki said.

'It's started now – just in time – but it doesn't look very happy. Oh, no, now it's stopped at the first jump.'

'Poor rider, how awful to have a naughty horse with everyone watching.'

'I don't think they're going to get very far. Come on, let's head for the wood,' Niki said, getting up.

The girls walked on, exclaiming over the height and width of the jumps, discussing the ditches and banks, commenting on the differing styles of riding as horses galloped past them. They followed the winding track through the woods, and gasped at the size of the 'rider frightener' corner jumps.

'Thank goodness Summer is used to these so Anna won't be nervous,' Beth said.

'Yes, and she's made us practise over poles set up as

corners when we jump in the manège at home, so we know how to do them too,' Niki reminded her.

They spent several minutes watching at the water jump, mischievously rather hoping to see someone fall off and get wet.

'Uh oh look at the time. We'd better run so we don't keep Anna waiting.'

24

'You two go and look at the dressage scores while I run back to the trailer. Don't talk loudly remember, and check how many have lower marks than Anna,' Niki commanded her sisters before leaving them near the secretary's tent.

'Come on, Lolly. Do you remember which class she's in?' Beth grabbed Lolly's hand as they wriggled through the crowd around the score boards.

'I think she's moved up to Novice,' Lolly replied, trying to keep her voice low. 'Look, that board has N for Novice on it.' Being only 6, Lolly couldn't read very well.

'Well done, now look for A for Anna or S for

Summer,' Beth said as they stood in front of the large score board which showed all the dressage results and some of the show jumping marks.

Lolly tugged Beth's sleeve, whispering, 'Look, there's Anna,' she pointed, moving her finger along the line. 'She's got 28 and 0. That's good isn't it?'

'Yes, it's very good. Now see how many have less than 28. One, two – that's all – just two,' Beth replied, also whispering. 'And one of those has 4 in the jumping.'

They ducked out of the tent, 'What do we tell her? Last year Granny said we mustn't say she's winning, but she needs to know she's doing well,' Lolly said breathlessly as they ran to the lorry park.

'We'll say she had a really good dressage score of 28 and there are two others below her. But don't tell her one has jumping faults. That way she'll feel good about the dressage and know she still needs to go clear but won't take risks,' Beth decided.

Anna had already mounted and was ready to make her way to the start of the cross country course.

'Anna, oh, Anna, you've got a score of 28, and there are only a couple of others under 30,' Beth gasped. 'Not all the show jumping marks are up though.'

'Wow, thanks for that,' Anna laughed delightedly, patting the horse. 'I thought it was a good test but that has broken our record. Do you hear that Summer? Girl done good.'

'You took your time,' Niki said crossly. 'Help me put everything away so we can lock up before following.'

The girls picked up boots, brushes and headcollar, drink bottles and sandwich boxes, then Niki locked the Land Rover and all three ran after Anna, dodging between the parked horse lorries to catch up.

Anna walked around the warm up area letting Summer look about her and take in the atmosphere before asking her to canter, gently stretching her muscles after her rest. Niki went to the steward to check whether they were running to time, then carefully stood where Anna could see her.

'They're pretty much on time so you've got about 15 minutes,' she said, checking her watch.

'Thanks. Keep an eye on the starter and hold up 5 fingers when there are five riders before me, then 3, then wave when it's only one.'

'Niki, we'll head over to that little mound again. We'll be able to see most of the course from there, as well as the start, and it's out of the way of the horses,' Beth said, grabbing Lolly's hand.

'I'll join you when she goes to the start box,' Niki replied importantly.

Niki stayed near the steward, listening to conversations between other riders and their grooms, and keeping a close eye on the number of riders before Anna.

'You're a bit young to be a groom, aren't you?' commented the steward.

'Anna's usual groom couldn't come today,' Niki answered, crossing her fingers that Granny wouldn't mind being labelled a groom.

'Well, you're obviously doing a good job. I can tell I won't have to worry about whether your rider's ready,' the steward answered.

As instructed, Niki positioned herself where Anna could see her and held up three fingers as she came close.

'Have you checked your girth?' she called, remembering what Granny said.

Anna slowed to a walk, bending down to feel her girth before nodding and then continuing her warm up routine. Anna kept a close eye on Niki so when the girl turned away from the steward and waved, she made her way to the start box.

'Thanks Niki. See you later.'

'Good luck.'

Niki waited while the starter counted down the seconds.

'10, 9, 8, (Anna was circling the start box), 7, 6, 5, (she pushed Summer into a trot) 4, 3, 2 (they entered the box) 1, GO' and Summer cantered out of the start box towards the first jump, already in her stride.

Niki ran to the knoll, watching as Summer cleared the second and third jumps before disappearing into the trees. She reached Beth and Lolly as the pair came into view again, powering towards a double of logs and a wide flat jump called a table before skipping down a tricky downhill step combination.

The commentator had been following their progress, 'Anna Elliot on Summer is safely over the first three and heading into the trees; they've jumped 4 in good style and are going well through the woods and over the double logs. Now we have another starter on the course. Anna is coming back into view, and steadying up for the steps which they've taken in their stride.'

The sisters watched excitedly as their aunt galloped towards them, slowing down so she could take the corner jumps accurately, making sure Summer didn't miss them. Lolly was jumping too, up and down in excitement, 'Come on Anna, come on Summer.'

'Shh, stop bouncing, be quiet,' ordered Niki. 'You'll put them off if they see you.'

They could hear Summer's heavy breathing as she passed them, the hoof beats reaching a crescendo as she drew close, then fading again as she passed. Anna's face was set in a frown of concentration as she crouched over her horse's shoulders, guiding her with gentle movements of her hands, her legs firmly clamped to the horse's sides.

'Good girl, turn now, steady, steady...' her calm voice carried towards them.

The girls ran towards the finish, listening to the commentary and watching as Anna took the water jump. A huge splash heralded her entry into the lake, alarming the jump judges and making the spectators laugh. Summer bounded through the water before neatly skipping up the bank, over the narrow jump just one stride later.

'Come on Summer,' cried Niki, 'Only two more to go.'

'Wow, she's gone clear again. Wicked,' Beth gasped as they ran to meet her.

'Don't think she'll have any time penalties either. She gained on the horse in front and the one following is way back,' Niki agreed. 'I bet she's won the class.'

'She won her class last year too,' Lolly said.

'Yes, but that was only 100cm high. This time she's in the Novice class and the jumps are bigger, 110 cm high, wider and more technical too,' Niki explained, just as Anna had to her.

At last they caught up with Anna who had dismounted and was leading Summer around to cool down.

'That was super, Anna, the commentator said you

went clear and didn't think you had any time faults,' Niki said approaching her grinning aunt.

'She was fantastic. What a horse! That was just so much fun; she didn't put a foot wrong.' Anna patted and hugged her horse, who snorted, cracking her nostrils and butting her head against Anna's shoulder.

25

'Phew, I'm exhausted,' Anna said, wriggling out of her body protector and taking off her hat and gloves. 'Better wash her down straight away, then she can have her haynet.' The girls rushed around, filling a bucket with water, finding the sponge, collecting the wet and dirty tack to put into the back of the Land Rover, fetching a drink and sandwich for Anna, and generally tidying everything away.

At last everything was shipshape; Summer was happily munching on her hay; Anna was relaxing with a whole packet of Jaffa cakes and the girls were lounging on the rug with chocolate spread sandwiches, talking about the competition.

The tannoy coughed into life. 'The prize giving for the Novice Class will be in front of the Secretary's Tent in half an hour.'

'Can we come with you please?' Beth asked.

'Someone will need to stay with Summer. I'm sorry Niki, but would you mind? Beth and Lolly are both too young to be left alone with her.'

Niki's face fell. She was proud that Anna had relied on her today, but she desperately wanted to go too.

'Excuse me, I couldn't help overhearing,' a lady popped her head out of the next door lorry. 'If you like, I can keep an eye on your horse at the same time as I watch ours. We haven't done well enough to win anything today but won't be leaving yet.'

'Oh that would be really kind. Let me give you my mobile number in case of problems,' Anna smiled and Niki beamed at her.

'Thank you so much. We know Anna had a really good dressage score and then went clear in both the show jumping and cross country, so she stands a good chance of being placed, and I do so want to see her collect her prize,' she explained.

'My, that is exciting; especially against so many professional riders,' the lady replied.

Anna put on a clean shirt and johds and picked up her hat before giving Summer a last pat, telling her to behave herself, as she and the girls set off to look at the scores before the official prize giving.

'Can we have a wander round the stalls?'

'And buy an ice cream?'

'Yes, as long as you can eat it without getting messy. We have to be neat and tidy for the presentation.'

There was quite a crowd around the score board, but Lolly managed to wriggle through to the front where she quickly found Anna's name again.

'Come and look Anna,' she called, beckoning the others.

'Wow. You've finished on your dressage score – that's great,' Niki exclaimed, delighted that she remembered the jargon from last summer.

'Gosh, Summer has done well, hasn't she? There are only two better than us at dressage, and only one of them has gone clear too. It looks as though I might be second. That's so fantastic at our first go at this level,' Anna was very pleased.

'You've beaten loads of professional riders too,' Niki said, reading out some very well known names.

'They'll have been riding young and novice horses rather than their international ones, but yes, it's very satisfying. In fact, it's amazing and I'm dead chuffed, but keep that quiet, won't you,' Anna said as they left to buy ice creams and inspect the tack stalls. 'I could do with some new studs, is there anything you want to buy?'

'I'd like a tie pin like Niki bought last year,' Beth said counting her pocket money. 'What about you Lolly?'

'Another ice cream,' Lolly said decidedly. 'And I like those socks with the fat ponies on them.'

'Yes, they're fun aren't they. What about a matching pencil case or set of pens?'

'Mmm, a pencil case would be good for school to remind me of our lovely horsey holidays.'

The girls happily browsed until it was time for the presentation when they gathered in an excited huddle, clapping politely as the rosettes were handed out, beginning at the rider placed eighth and working up towards the winner. At last Anna's name was called out 'Second place is Anna Elliott on her home bred horse Summer. She also wins the Best Placed Local Rider prize and the Highest Placed at her first competition at this level.'

The girls clapped and cheered as a grinning Anna went up to collect her three rosettes, a smart rug for Summer, a silver cup and a sash.

'Wow, what a lot you won,' Lolly exclaimed, grabbing hold of the cup as they politely clapped the actual winner, a professional who dashed off quickly as he still had more horses to ride.

A young lady with a notepad and pen stopped Anna.

'Excuse me,' she said. 'I represent Horse and Hound magazine. Can I interview you and take some pictures? Tell me, what does it feel like to come second at your first Novice event?'

'Oh, well, I still can't really believe it,' Anna answered. 'We bred my horse from my mother's mare who I used to event with the Pony Club. Summer hasn't been the easiest, as she thinks she knows best and doesn't always listen but today she was brilliant, even when a little dog chased us on the cross country course. And my nieces have been really great grooms – they've made everything run smoothly.'

'They look a bit young to be really helpful.'

'Well, normally my mother grooms for me but she couldn't come today, and rather than miss my local competition the girls promised to help. They've even given up a day of riding their own ponies to help me.'

'Oh, so you're all riders? Do you compete too?'

'We already compete with Pony Club, jumping and stuff, but I can't wait until I can do cross country. It looks so much fun,' Niki replied.

'My pony is really obedient. She's a good jumper but I like dressage best,' Beth said shyly.

'I like jumping and going fast and I'm off the lead rein now. I'd love to ride Summer one day,' Lolly said.

'Wow, I can see I'll have to remember your names, it sounds as though you'll be the next generation of famous riders.'

'Come on kids, let's take Summer home.'

'Can I ring Granny on your phone please and tell her how well you've done?' Beth asked.

'Have we really been helpful?' Niki asked, feeling very pleased.

'Yes, you really have. You've collected numbers, made sure I've been in the right place at the right time, and generally been cheerful putting things away and keeping me calm. I'm very grateful to all three of you,' Anna answered, high fiveing her nieces.

'Now let's get Summer loaded and go home so you can help clean my tack,' she added with a grin, making them all groan.

'P'raps Daddy and Mummy will have arrived,' Lolly said hopefully.

'If you think that'll get you out of the chores . . .' Anna remarked, laughing.

'Oh no, we'll all help, won't we, Lolly,' Niki said, nudging her sister. 'I'm looking forward to seeing them too, only . . . it means it's nearly time to go home, and back to school, and that's not so much fun.' Niki suddenly looked upset.

'Never mind, you've a couple more days yet, and

the whole summer holidays to look forward to.' Anna gave her a hug.

'Wagons roll,' she added, and they all jumped into the car, happy to be heading home to one of Granny's special suppers.